RAT WAR
A HORROR ANTHOLOGY
EDITED BY
ANTHONY GIANGREGORIO

Rat War: A Horror Anthology

RAT WAR

EDITED BY
ANTHONY GIANGREGORIO

Table of Contents

A SPECIAL PLACE

SCOTT WIECZOREK

New York City – 1932

Goddamn it, Vic thought as he ran even faster, *these cops are quick!*

And they were. The police had been chasing him for about five blocks now. and were starting to close in on him, but he knew that in just a few quick turns he could find safety from them.

Vic turned right down the alley next to a bakery and then ditched left into a narrow alleyway behind the same building. Darting behind a small projection from the back of the building, he was obscured from sight. Pressing himself against the wall, he held his breath and strained his ears to listen for the footsteps of the police officers pursuing him.

One…two…three…four…

Wait. There were at least five cops chasing him. Had the others broken off to run down the main road? Had he miscounted? No, he was sure there were more than four cops chasing him. But where had the others gone?

Then he heard them. Five…six…

But then there was something else—a slower set of footsteps. These were walking…seven. He breathed out slowly, now feeling the effects of holding his breath for so long. Then another set of footsteps joined in.

These cops were going far too slow to be part of the chase. They were sweeping—checking to make sure he hadn't turned off somewhere along the path.

Vic scanned his surroundings. He'd been behind the bakery many times in the past and knew the layout well. There were trash cans to his right, a fire-escape above him, and a manhole cover leading into the sewer at his feet.

He knew the cops would easily find him if he tried climbing the fire escape; not to mention that his footsteps would resonate on the metal, and if he was stupid enough to duck behind the cans, Vic knew that he would ultimately stand up to find himself looking into the business end of one of the cops' service revolvers.

No, the only way out for him was down.

So far, the footsteps were still out in the main alleyway. He could hear the two cops talking in the alley beyond. The voices were faint, as if they were being whispered, but he could still hear them.

Voice 1: "I can't wait to get my paws on that crook!"

Voice 2: "Yeah, I know what ya mean. There's a special place in hell for a thief like him."

Voice 1: "Yeah. No kiddin', huh? Not to mention what the boys'd do to him in the lockup."

Voice 2: "Vermin like him'll get their comeuppance one way or another."

Vic smiled, and thought, *Hell, Schmell. Ya ain't catchin' me, coppers*. But he knew that he didn't have long to wait before the police would be making their way down the alley. He knelt down slowly. There was a small piece of pavement missing on one side of the manhole cover, from where the last sewer worker had pried it off with a tool. It was just large enough for Vic to get his fingers in and pry the manhole cover up. Straining with the effort and weight of the heavy lid, he gripped the heavy cover with both hands and pulled with all his might.

It moved, but only a little. Putting his knees and legs into it, he was able to lever the edge of the lid up a little more and shove it gently out of the way. He tied the canvas sack he was clutching in his hands around the piece of rope he used for a belt, and slowly slipped through the narrow opening into the manhole below. With luck, he quickly managed to find the iron rungs attached to the inside of the shaft.

With his shoulder and one hand, he lifted the lid a fraction and slid it back into place; it seated with a dull sound. His only hope was that the noise of the cast iron lid falling into the metal ring of the manhole shaft wasn't too loud. He decided there wasn't anything he could do about it. If it had attracted the cops' attention, then he needed to make sure he put as much distance between himself and the police as humanly possible.

The sewer in which he found himself had a low ceiling, about four-and-a half feet high. It forced him to crouch low while walking; it was very dark. But tracing his footsteps back toward the larger alley brought him to a slightly bigger arched-brick pipe, where he only had to stoop a little. It also had a little light filtering in from the right side. Making a right, he soon found himself in the main junction of the sewer, which ran underneath the street on which he'd been running on earlier.

The junction to the sewer was interesting in its design. The bottom had two flat platforms running the length of the brick pipe along the outer edges, while toward the middle it was concave, making a channel through which the offal could flow. The walls were about four feet-high on each side and connected to a high-arched ceiling.

Vic marveled at the thought of how much sewage could flow through the pipe at one time—it must have been millions of gallons per hour. At the moment, there was only a slight trickle of waste running through the lowest portion of the center channel, which was a good thing.

Suffuse light filtered into the sewer through the storm drain openings on the left and right along the edge of the street. Given the faint trickle of waste flowing through today, he was pleasantly surprised that the odor wasn't too bad. He checked out his shoes, not remembering if he had worn his old ones, or the ones he had lifted from a bum he'd beaten up that morning.

He wore the new ones, so at least his feet would stay pretty dry. He smiled, pleased with the fact that he'd given the police the slip. *Stupid coppers*, he thought. *They won't even think of checkin' the sewers for hours. By then, I'll be long gone.*

He heard something move behind him and his heart leapt into his throat. Surely, he'd spoken too soon. He turned around slowly, expecting to see one of the officers covering him with his gun.

Instead, Vic saw the sinister red glowing eyes of a handful of sewer rats. He laughed out loud and then caught himself, not wanting to give away his location to any cops that could hear on the street above.

Only some stupid rats, he thought. *Nothing to be scared of here.*

Finding a small stone on the floor of the sewer, he flicked it at the cluster of little scavengers and watched them scatter, chittering and squealing loudly as they ran. The stone clicked across the sewer floor and it landed and bounced into the darkness.

That'll teach ya, he thought with a smile and a quiet laugh.

Vic stood on the right-hand platform and began making his way in the same direction of the street, back in the direction he was originally headed before he ducked down the alley and then into the sewer. As he walked, visions filled his head of just what he was going to do with his loot. This was his first big boost, and to think that all this cash came from an orphanage. He usually stuck to small banks with inept guards, but this time he'd managed to dupe the ladies at the orphanage out of the contents of the entire safe with some fake dynamite sticks. He'd told them he'd throw one into the kids' rooms as they slept.

When he'd first gotten the fake sticks from his sister for Christmas, she was so proud of her first attempt at making candles. But the damn things were just so weird looking. That was when it hit him—they looked just like real dynamite sticks. So, that's what he'd use them for. He lit them and used them to intimidate his marks. In his dreams, the ploy had worked easily, and he was even more ecstatic when it worked in reality as well. He would have to remember to give his sister a big kiss the next time he saw her. Maybe he'd even take her with him when he left the city to buy his own little farm out in the country. After all, isn't that what family did? This score was his salvation. His family's as well.

Vic hadn't been paying too much attention to how far he'd walked. He knew that he had quite a way to go, but it slowly occurred to him that he had no idea where he was. Underground in the sewer, it was hard to estimate how far he'd actually gone. He guessed that he must have only walked a few streets, and turned around to look for any familiar landmarks from when he first entered the sewer.

Behind him, he was surprised by what he actually saw. Scores upon scores of rats were skulking behind him. They remained at a safe distance, about a dozen or so paces away, but were packed into a tight group. Vic guessed there had to be at least fifty or so of the little rodents, their evil-looking red eyes staring up at him in unison.

Having spent most of his life growing up in the city's tenements, Vic had had more than his share of run-ins with rats. But usually, there were only one or two at the most, and they were never as well organized as this. Typically, they'd be alone and rooting through a cupboard or some trash bin. But this was something else altogether.

He had to admit that their behavior made him a little nervous. Still, they were just rats. He picked up another loose stone and threw it into their midst, pleased to see them scatter again. The stone didn't click this time and instead he heard a dull, meaty thud. He must have hit one of them. What luck.

"Ha," he said, "serves ya right, ya little bastards!"

Forgetting why he had turned around in the first place, he started walking forward again, only this time he quickened his pace.

Trying to distract himself from the rats' odd behavior, he thought instead of the small farm he'd seen for sale on the outskirts of town. It was a nice little place, only about fifty or so acres. He figured he could probably handle that himself without needing to hire any hands. If he raised some hogs and goats, he could sell their pelts for cash. He could make himself a nice little farmstead for himself and his sister with this one heist. Then he could give up the life. No more stealing, pinching, or doing some other thug's dirty work. He would go on the straight and narrow. He might even give up the booze. Now that would make his sister happy.

He figured he must have walked several more streets. Out the corners of his eyes, he could see that many of the smaller intersecting sewer pipes were occupied by rats. There must have been a breeze blowing through one of the storm grates as he passed because suddenly a chill ran down his spine. He wasn't the kind of man to spook easy, but these rats were making the little hairs on the back of his neck stand on end.

Vic stopped in an attempt to gather his bearings. He knew that the pipe had turned slightly a little ways back, but remembered that the direction he wanted to follow was straight as an arrow from downtown to uptown.

I might be gettin' a little off the beaten path, here, he thought, then resolved to pop his head up into one of the storm grates to figure out where he was.

He stepped over to one of the niches in the ceiling where the grates were set, reached his hands up to grab the grate, and pulled himself up to see the world outside the sewer. As his nose rose up above the iron grate, his eyes came up level with a pair of red orbs.

"Sonofabitch!" he yelled and relinquished his grasp on the grate. As his feet hit the slick brick floor beneath him, they slipped out from under him. His back struck the wall of the sewer and his head was knocked heavily into the brick, causing him to see stars. He toppled onto his side and struck his head again on the offal-covered floor. He flailed, pushing himself backward in an attempt to keep from slipping downward into the sewer channel where he might drown, and only barely managed to save himself from such a filthy fate.

"Blasted rats!" he exclaimed. "Go away! Lemme be!" His head was pounding and it felt wet. A touch to the back of his head confirmed that it was, indeed wet, and as his hand came into his blurred sight, it was evident that it was wet with blood.

Great, he thought, *damn rats almost made me break my neck.*

He looked around, feeling somewhat embarrassed at his reaction to the rat up on the grate, half expecting to see one of his mates from the neighborhood laughing at him, like they always seemed able to do. It never mattered where he was. Anytime he'd had a clumsy accident like this, one of his buddies had been there to rub it in but good. At least, he mused, none of them would be caught dead in a sewer. So, at least this time he was safe from ridicule.

Instead of finding his mates, however, his wandering eyes did pick up on some silent observers. In the sewer behind him, there now had to be more than two hundred rats. They were closer now, too, probably four or five paces from where Vic lay.

Vic closed his eyes momentarily in an attempt to clear his head and put a halt to the whirling stars dancing through his vision. When he opened them again, he noticed that the rats were only about a pace or two away. The rats lining the intersecting sewer across from him were also now standing on the raised platform instead of lining the interior of the pipe and staying to the darkness. He suddenly heard their chittering and squealing.

What the hell is going on with these things? he wondered. *It's almost like they're chasin' me, or somethin'.* The theory came upon him quickly and he dismissed it with equal speed as sheer paranoia over the prospect of getting caught after the heist. "You're just rats! You filthy, diseased vermin!" he yelled at them. "Get outta here!"

His hand reached out for another rock and closed on a brick this time. He picked it up and hurled it at the closest rat to him. As one, the entire mass of rats watched the brick while it flew through the air. Vic felt his hackles rise, watching all the rats act this way. The brick struck the rat he had targeted and crushed it instantly beneath the force of the blow. Then, in unison, all of the tiny red eyes turned their attention back to him.

Vic's stomach leapt to his throat and he scrambled to his knees. He needed to get out of the sewer. There was something seriously wrong. Rats shouldn't be acting this way. They were wild rats—they shouldn't be so in control.

All at once, the rats took one more step forward—toward him. He turned around, ready to keep forging ahead down the sewer and away from these bizarre rodents. His few steps forward were matched by tiny steps from the massive body of rats following him. He could see now that they really were following him.

"Leave me be, ya lousy beasts," he yelled at the growing crowd behind him. "I ain't no Pied Piper, so be gone with ya!" The rats simply continued following him. Apparently, they didn't understand him.

As he passed each intersection, he noticed that more and more rats were piling into the main section. It ultimately came to the point where Vic needed to find creative ways to step around them on the raised platform he was traveling on.

He couldn't tell how long he'd been wandering along the sewer pipe, but when he came to a split in the path ahead, he needed to decide whether to go left or right. He knew from walking along the streets above that he needed to follow to the right, but as he approached the turn, the sewer pipe became filled with the dreadful chittering and squealing of more rats.

"Damn it!" he yelled at them. "Get the hell out of my way!" He reached for a nearby brick lying nearby and yelped in pain when he was bitten on the side of the hand by a nearby rat. He cursed out loud and kicked at the rodent, but it simply stood on its hind legs and stared at him with its vile red eyes. Angry now, Vic kicked out again and this time connected with the defiant little rat, sending it flying through the air only to spatter against the wall with a sound that reminded him of his father slapping a freshly cut steak on the cutting table in the butcher shop. Immediately, all around him erupted a roar of chitters and squeals, and as he looked around, he could see nearly a thousand pairs of angry red eyes fixated on him.

"I'll kill each and every one of ya!" he bellowed in rage. "Now, ya best git out of my way if ya know what's good for ya!" He decided to try and stomp off along the path to the right, but was deterred when the solid mass of rats moved to stop his attempt. So, instead of trying to get around the rats, he swung his legs in great arcs in an attempt to bull his way through them. Unfortunately, his attack only incited them to more violence against him. Every time his leg swung into the sea of dark fur, a dozen or so rats would attach themselves to his leg with their razor-sharp claws and sink their teeth into his legs.

He screamed out in pain and swatted at his legs to shake the little rodents off him. But their jaws were strong and some of them took chunks of meat from his legs with them as he tried to pull the rats off and cast them aside. Some of the faster ones also leaped from his legs to his arms and continued their attack.

Vic stumbled in pain and fell backward, sprawling onto the floor. Once there, the rats suddenly stopped their assault and returned to their places in the seething mass of vermin blocking access to his one path of escape.

He didn't know why, but he suddenly thought, *How do they know which way I need to take?*

It made no sense. These creatures didn't know who he was. They knew nothing about him. But yet, they knew exactly which way he wanted to go. They knew his way home.

"What's goin' on here?" he asked them, despite knowing they couldn't answer him. They were rats. Simple, mindless, filthy rats!

He tried again to ford through the mass of rodents, but again they assaulted him, chewing on his legs. Despite that he tried to run away, the rats around his feet caused him to fall face first into them. The landing was surprisingly pleasant, when instead of striking the cold and hard brick floor, he landed into warm, soft fur. But the pleasantness disappeared quickly as the rodents swarmed over his head and back biting and clawing at his neck and face.

He screamed in terror, his body experiencing an endorphin rush that masked the pain of the hundreds of bites, and he scrambled back to the platform where the rats again ceased their assault on him. "What the…! Get offa me, you filthy little bastards! Get off!" Vic bellowed at the horde of rats like he'd never yelled before in his life. "So, ya want me goin' this way? Well, fine then! I'll go this way. Just ya stop you're bitin', ya filthy trash!"

The rats stared at him, but didn't move as long as he was standing on the platform. Vic hung his head and started down the left sewer pipe. He could see that the rats were coming in closer, only a step or two off now, and the swarm was growing. It was as if the ones following him thus far had joined with the attackers from the right pipe.

Vic didn't know if it was getting warmer, or if the sewer gas was getting to him, but he was starting to sweat. No, he had to admit it to himself, he was getting scared. These rats were acting strange and they were corralling him. He was like a cow being driven to the cattle-puncher, only, he didn't know for what purpose.

The sewer pipe began to slope steeply downward and suddenly became much slicker. Vic had a hard time keeping his footing on the slime-covered brick. About midway down, he lost his balance and fell over backward, smacking his head smartly on the platform and rolling into the center channel carrying the offal from the city above. Stars again swam around his head and his consciousness slipped into inky blackness.

He woke to the sound of chittering and squealing. His eyes were blurry and he could barely see in the darkness surrounding him. But he could tell that he wasn't lying where he had fallen before passing out. Below him, he could feel carpeting; the floor was soft and warm. But there was warmth from somewhere else nearby as well. He turned his head to the left and could see a flicker of light. There was a fire.

His eyes slowly adjusted to the light in the room. The fire was growing larger and his surroundings became clearer. All around him were thousands upon thousands of pairs of glowing red eyes, and they were all focused on him. He tried to sit up, but found that he was somehow unable to move. It was as if something was holding him to the floor. Vic lifted his head a little and could see that he had been tied up.

Oddly, the chittering and squealing he was hearing took on a sudden cadence from which he could discern a definite pattern. It was almost like the rats were chanting. All at once, the red eyes turned away from him and looked to something in the distance before him. As he absorbed the scene around him, Vic saw that he was in a large, underground cavern of some type with literally millions of rats.

The rats he could see were all standing on their hind legs, and seemed to be bowing rhythmically in time with the chant toward the front of the cavern, as though in supplication.

A massive shadow moved across the far wall of the cavern. It looked rat-like, but also had many human qualities to it. Vic didn't have to wait long to discover what made such an odd shadowy image, as the creature suddenly came into view.

Vic tried to turn his head away from the massive horror which was before him, but found that as with his body, something held his head fast in place. Instead, he closed his eyes tightly. But as he did this, little claws grasped at his eyelids and pried them open. He had no other choice but to view the abomination at the front of the cavern.

It was easily the size of a man, if not larger, and appeared to be a grotesque hybrid between human and rat. Its head had an elongated snout and two large ears. The body was bulbous and misshapen around the midsection, the legs were short and stout, and the arms were abnormally long and thin with claw-like fingers. The musculature on the beast looked very much human though it had little, if any hair.

The massive rat-man stepped up onto a stone dais located near the far wall and sat down on a chair that was barely visible through the flames of the fire. The rhythmic chittering was rising to a crescendo, when all of a sudden the rat-man raised its hands. A hush fell across the mass of rodents.

"Ra-ch-ch-(squeal)-ch-ch-ra." The rat-man said to the horde of vermin. Its voice was deep and authoritative. At once, all of the supplicant rats began to mimic its vocalization, and it was just then that Vic realized that the carpet beneath him had begun to writhe and move.

It's not a carpet. I'm layin' on bloody rats! Vic thought. He screamed as he realized that the mass of vermin which his body lay on was ushering him forward toward the man-rat on the dais. Vic tried to resist, but his body was bound tight and he was powerless to stop any momentum.

The closer he moved toward the rat-man on the dais, the more panic set in. His mind was reeling. Then panic gave way to sheer and utter fear as the rat-man began speaking to him.

"Human," the rat-man said in perfect English, "We, the children of Ra-ch-ch-(squeal)-ch-ch-ra, bestow upon you the great honor of being the venerable guest of Ra-ch-ch-(squeal)-ch-ch-ra, the Great Old One." A chorus of seemingly jubilant squeals resounded through the chamber, and just like the Red Sea that was parted by Moses, so did the vast sea of rats before Vic divide in two. Behind him, Vic could hear something shuffling, but he was unable to turn his head to see what was coming. From what he could hear, it sounded big. As he watched, the space between the two columns of parted rats spread twenty-feet in width.

Accompanying the shuffling, Vic could now hear something else. It was the sound of deep, labored breathing and heavy slobbering. He desired nothing more at this point in time than to turn his head to the right to see what he presumed to be some primordial horror lurking near him, but the bindings which held him tightened with every move of his limbs. The sound continued its approach at a painfully slow pace. It seemed like an eternity had passed by the time that he saw the back of what he assumed to be the 'Great Old One' pass by him.

From what he could see, the thing was massive. Its back was at least ten-feet in breadth and its hunched form must have stood more than twelve-feet tall. Vic didn't want to see that form stretch to its full height, which he surmised must be more than twenty-feet. Behind it the thing dragged a thick muscular tail that at its smallest part was thicker than Vic's leg. To Vic's best estimation, the thing must have been a rat of massive size. But as it reached the dais and turned around, Vic saw that he could not be any further from the truth.

Granted the 'Great Old One' had aspects similar to a rat, such as a wiry tail, a thick powerful neck, and a rat's head and snout, but that was where the similarities stopped. The eyes weren't red like a normal rat, but instead appeared to be completely milky-white, and its ears appeared to look more human than rat-like. Where there should have been a bulbous rat body was instead a wide, gaping maw ringed with hundreds of long, sharp teeth. It reminded Vic of a hole-saw he had once seen while working as a laborer in a carpenters shop, except it was more like a hundred such saws of various sizes, all nested within each other. Outside of the massive maw were hundreds of tentacle-like appendages flailing about. The place where the thing's massive chest should have been was occupied by more than a dozen pairs of eyes, all arranged in random positions and orientation, which scanned all around, some blinking and some not.

Vic began to laugh at the absurdity of the thing standing on the dais before him. That it could exist was a distinct impossibility. Surely, he was dreaming. That's it, he'd been knocked unconscious while trying to elude the police and now his mind was running wild. His laughter, however, was short-lived and quickly turned over to cries of anguish as the tentacles burrowed into his flesh. He felt them beneath his skin, writhing inside his abdomen like a hundred snakes. The endorphins his brain released could do nothing to stop the tide of pain growing in his body as the tenta-cles began pulling apart great sections of his skin, fat, and muscle.

He could feel a sharp, burning sensation in his anus as one of the tentacles retracted from his abdomen, carrying with it what seemed to Vic to be a long sausage casing.

That's funny, he thought as the pain overwhelmed him. *Where'd that all come from? I didn't eat any sausage.*

Laughter again broke from Vic's blood-coated lips as droplets of crimson splattered across the dais and the monstrosity before him. The chittering behind him once more began to rise to a crescendo and he decided to join in the chant of cheering on the 'Great Old One,' of whom he was the venerated guest. As his mind cracked and he embraced the pain, and just before consciousness slipped away from him, Vic let the divine ecstasy which was overtaking him fill his body. He thought back to his sister, to the orphans from whom he'd stolen the money, and to the police he'd eluded. He had no desire or need for them anymore. This was where he belonged, in the 'Great Old One's' embrace, amidst his brethren.

He was home.

ANDY'S CHAINS

ROBERT DUBUQUE

"**W**ill, I'm going up to the attic, do you wanna come?" Shannon asked.

I was sitting on the back deck with a nearly empty Foster's, enjoying the sunset. But I always made time for my family.

I got up out of my comfy patio lounger. I'd probably have only a couple more weeks before I had to put it away for the winter. We were enjoying an Indian summer in New England this year, but whenever an Indian summer is over, we really gotta pay for it. Typically with a couple of feet of the white stuff, no electricity, and a snowblower that worked perfectly in March, but won't even make an effort to start now.

I opened the screen door and walked into the kitchen. My wife was standing on the other side of the room holding a bucket.

"What's on the menu tonight, hon?" I asked, like I did every night.

"Well, the soup of the day is an autumn blend of last night's turkey bones, coffee grounds, and various citrus fruit peels, topped with a gravy of beer swill you crushed your Marlboro into," she replied with a smirk on her face.

I could smell it from across the room.

Without another word she turned around and walked into the living room, bumping the bucket on the T.V. stand and getting some of the smelly mixture on the hardwood floor. I decided to clean it up after dinner.

I walked behind Shannon up the stairs, admiring the view her yoga pants afforded me. I would've reached out and given her a pinch, but I wouldn't want her to spill the soup in surprise. There was carpet on the stairs. I didn't see that smell coming out too easily.

At the top of the stairs she pulled the keys to the Master lock out of her shirt pocket as she set the metal bucket on the ground. She stood on her tiptoes and unlocked it and the latch swung down off the attic's trap door. I reached over her and yanked on the string, careful not to brain my wife in the process.

The well-maintained attic stairs slid all the way down to the carpet with barely a sound. Well-oiled, well-used, and even the bottom of the ladder was muffled on the thick white carpet. I gave Shannon the ladies first gesture. She did a mock curtsy and grabbed the bucket with the hand that was supposed to be daintily lifting her imaginary gown. She shimmied between the ladder and the wall, careful not to spill the contents in the bucket. I followed suit.

At the top of the attic stairs was a light switch. She flicked it as soon as it was within reach. Shannon rocked backwards and I quickly popped up a step to hold her steady, and a few drops of the concoction slopped over the side onto my jeans. I'd have to buy a new pair. Fermented cigarette beer isn't a smell that comes out.

Shannon leaned her lower back against the attic floor, never making her way all the way up, never making a noise. When I walked past her I could feel fear radiating from her body like electricity.

I stood up in the attic and surveyed the situation. Broken chains were still strapped to the support beam and there were chew marks on nearly every possible surface. Even blood in many places. I had to assume it was Andy's blood. And the worst sight in the whole room was a hole in the wall, Andy's claw marks surrounding it.

"Oh shit, he got out. He got out. Oh shit." I kept repeating over and over again. I'd feared this day for six years. I was experiencing empty nest syndrome about twelve years too early.

They'll always thrive on this planet. Forget the cockroaches. Rats aren't meek. They'll inherit the earth.

I grew up in Wholeton, Massachusetts. It was a hole. The typical 'There used to be a prosperous mill here but now we're all tanked 24/7' type of town.

Vermin, to me, would be a creature that takes one bad turn of luck—like losing a shitty job at a malodorous peanut factory—and says to itself "Fuck it, some liquor stores accept food stamps for booze." A rat wouldn't drown itself in Rebel Yell because one food source had been depleted. They'd find nutrition elsewhere.

I developed this rather unconventional opinion toward the small—and sometimes not so small—opportunists after witnessing my father's rage towards them one day.

In our western Mass. shack we had only three rooms and an outhouse. It was 1996. Indoor plumbing was not exactly cutting edge technology. The shack consisted of my room, my parents' room, and a kitchen. The kitchen had one corner boxed off with plywood that my mother deemed 'The Pantry.' It was rarely stocked.

That month, my father had found a couple days of work doing routine maintenance and minor repairs on a fleet of old Isuzu box trucks for a paper recycling company two towns over. For once, our food stamps were actually spent on food and not crappy whiskey that costs as much as gas if you buy it by the gallon.

It was another nice Indian summer, high seventies despite Thanksgiving creeping up the next week. My father went to the pantry, obviously deciding that he couldn't subside totally on semi-flammable liquid. I was sitting in the kitchen when my dad yelled in slightly slurred speech as he opened the door, "God-damned *vahmints*, you wanna fuck with my family!" His thick New England accent seemed at odds with the fact that the word 'varmints' hadn't been used since just after the Emancipation Proclamation.

My father lifted his right boot, the one with the hole on the inner toe, and brought it down violently as many as two dozen times. I knew what he was squashing. I'd seen the rat's nest in there before. Half of me was in shock at the fact that he was killing a living, breathing family of animals. The other half was happy in a sick kind of way. It was nice to see that boot hurt someone who wasn't his son.

He finished stomping and walked out of the room, clearly suffering from ILS—invisible lat syndrome. He thought he was a tough guy.

When I knew he had returned to the backyard and his bottle of Rebel Yell, I went to survey the damage. All the baby rats were smooshed beyond recognition. Their eyes were popped out and their bodies were a mess of bloody, miscolored red. But I didn't see the mother rat. She was a big girl, too, I wouldn't have missed her despite the devastation of my dad's worn-out, knock-off Timberlands. She must have been out gathering food for the babies.

The next day I was checking 'The Pantry' for food, with an expected sense of disappointment. I knew there would be no food. For a first grade student, I was right a lot.

What I wasn't so disappointed to see was the mother rat. She was inspecting the leftovers of my mother's half-assed cleaning job of the rat family; bloodstains and dried guts that weren't so well hidden in the corner of the makeshift food storage area. The mother rat knew better than to fear a good stomping from me, as we'd had several encounters and I never tried to hurt her.

She moved on.

I saw her a month later behind the outhouse with a new litter of babies. She still fed them, she still got herself fat so they could suckle. She had one family destroyed so she started a new one in a safer place, if a little less protected from the elements. I had respect for a creature that could see its family murdered and still push on towards the goal of species enhancement.

I left that shithole town but never forgot that mother rat. Her defiance towards the top of the food chain was even mentioned in my college thesis about the Occupy Movement.

That mother rat always stuck with me.

But Shannon's upbringing didn't afford her the same affection towards the 'vermin.'

West Pondbury, Massachusetts. A town where everyone was for public assistance as long as the people who needed it were at least two towns over. A town where the domicile you lived in was a place you called home proceeded by a season.

How I ever landed her I don't know. A tattooed, chain-smoking, English major at UMass whose heavy drinking wasn't called alcoholism by virtue of atmosphere, doesn't typically take a bored business major to bed. Or to the altar.

Shannon had never seen a rat outside of a pet store in her life. If she had, I'd imagine she'd either vomit or faint like a 1950's TV housewife. Despite her lack of knowledge towards the furry survivors, I knew there was a hatred towards any scavengers, probably brought on by her silver-spoon upbringing. Once again, it was the idea that help was an admirable notion, as long as it could be distanced from the benefactors.

We had a whirlwind romance that started with Shannon wanting to make an effort to piss off her parents, and ended with me standing at the altar, wondering what the hell I was doing marrying a girl who should have a silver spoon in her mouth and not a criminal's tongue. I was arrested for possession when I was twenty, a substance that is now legal.

Long story short, we fell in love and bought a house together. Between my novels and semi-popular blog about environmental consciousness, and her trust fund—doled out on a yearly basis—we had a nice three-story home in a part of western Massachusetts that had never even heard about Wholeton.

Then we tried to have kids. For months we tried. No go. We must've spent more money on pregnancy tests than we did on food, but my swimmers just couldn't find their way to the pool. Then we saw a specialist.

Sitting in the waiting room, I had this selfish inner monologue where I was begging any powers that may be listening that I wasn't the one who was causing a lack of conception. It was very chauvinistic, I'll admit, but I didn't want to look at my wife and have her look back with eyes that said 'You're not a real man.'

Despite my atheistic ideals, my silent prayers were answered. Shannon was barren. There was a lot of technical speech about her uterus and fallopian tubes, but the doctor trying to explain that to me was like an English major trying to explain the sprouts of hope that McCarthy planted in *The Road* to a physics major writing his thesis on 'spooky action at a distance.' The bottom line was Shannon couldn't have her baby.

The wannabe grandma—Shannon's mom, not mine, who I hadn't even invited to my wedding—put up money and contacted all kinds of advanced fertility doctors. We tried it all. From me from changing briefs to boxers, to eating raw meats, we tried everything. Nothing took.

Shannon's mom, whom I affectionately referred to as Muffy, found a doctor in Germany who was trying new things with genetics. Like I said, I'm not a big science buff, but I got the idea that his experiments weren't precisely legal in the States.

Muffy paid big bucks for this guy. We flew to Germany and had a short consultation with him, our lack of German slightly less embarrassing than his lack of English, and then he started doing tests on Shannon, making sure she wouldn't be hurt by his extreme procedures. Apparently malpractice lawsuits are just as serious in Germany as they are in the U.S.

I was also given some pills to enhance my libido and to increase my sexual performance. We fucked like rabbits. Shannon spent her days in the lab with a creepy German doctor, and I spent my days 'doing research for my next novel,' which mostly included drinking beer and smoking European weed.

Nobody ever says that they can remember exactly when their baby was conceived, but I'm pretty sure I've got it down to the hour. Shannon and I went out for dinner and drinks. To this day I can swear I remember Dr. Mengele (not his real name) mentioning something about Shannon abstaining from alcohol, but she'll insist that no German has ever directed a person, regardless of nationality, away from a beer. But we were drunk.

So we stumbled back to our motel room, acquiring that obnoxious accent every New Englander starts re-using when they're tipsy, and went directly to bed. We stayed up all night, eating hotel food in between love-making sessions in preparation for the next go, and watching German versions of American cartoons. They also had a plentiful supply of German beer, drank warm, so as not to offend the invisible Krauts in the room.

We found out two days later that we would become a trio. Early detection had a different definition in German, apparently. We were overjoyed. Shannon made a long distance call to her mother in the States and they talked for hours.

Mengele insisted we stay in Germany through the pregnancy. He cited past cases and said there 'may or may not be unique complications due to the unusual conception.' I didn't mind, our child's citizenship would be easy enough to obtain once we were stateside again, but Shannon seemed a little concerned about having a baby in Europe.

She convinced me to leave. We had an appointment with the doctor the next day, but we left that night. We paid cash for a ticket back to Logan Airport, and were soon home again. We even had to change our cell numbers and emails because Mengele's office began harassing us, trying to make us comeback.

We got an OBGYN and a pediatric doctor. We said nothing to them about how Shannon got pregnant. We did the typical first pregnancy thing, buying stuff for the baby, going to classes on birthing, reading *What To Expect*, everything we could do that had anything to do with the baby.

There were no complications with the pregnancy. Shannon was sick about as often as a pregnant woman gets sick. She put on weight. She complained a lot and had constant cravings for Reese's and cake.

We were really looking forward to the twenty week check up. That's when we were going to find out if we were having a boy or a girl. Like most men, I wanted a little boy. I wanted to be the dad my father wasn't. I wanted to teach my little boy all the stuff I had to figure out on my own.

And like most women, Shannon wanted a little girl, to dress up. I swear that giving little girls dolls to play with is corporate America's way of conditioning our youth to want to be parents.

The day of our check-up came. Shannon wore her nicest maternity clothes and I tried to bear as little resemblance to a homeless man as possible. We knew it wasn't logical, but we wanted to look nice for the baby.

The ultrasound technician must have had the worst bedside manner in medical history. I realize it must have been shocking to see a fetus with a snout and a tail, but you would think someone who is supposed to be personable through one of the most impor-tant times in your life could do a little bit better than "What the hell..."

The baby had teeth. For some reason that was what blew my mind. Not the tail, not the snout, not the thick covering of hair that the doctor still insisted on calling *lanugo*. It was those tiny teeth lining the snout, somehow giving me the idea of sharpness despite a distinct lack in resolution on the ultrasound.

Shannon took it in stride. It was her little boy. She loved him and she didn't care. The heartless bastards at the doctor's office advised us to abort the pregnancy. I'm pro-choice. Shannon's pro-choice. But after the heartache we went through, all the trying, all we wanted to be was a family.

I was more distraught than Shannon. I would never have got-ten rid of my son, of course, but I just didn't see how a fetus that looked like *that* could be healthy.

"We can give him a good life. He's our miracle. We love each other and we can love him," Shannon would say. During the later parts of the pregnancy, she was quieter.

A regular OBGYN wasn't what we needed. Our little boy had to be kept a secret from everyone. The suggestions of abortion and the subtle hints from doctors about bringing in other specialists pissed us off. Then Muffy swooped in.

She shared the opinion with Shannon that love was all our child needed. My sweet mother-in-law hired a birthing coach for Shannon and we prepared for a home birth.

The birthing coach, Elsie, was over within fifteen minutes of me calling her. Despite everything, I think she may have been the best in the world at what she did. She was very new age, one of those people who 'aren't religious, but very spiritual' and one of the nicest women I've ever met.

Shannon was having contractions and that's why we called our new age birthing coach. I was a total wreck. We never told Elsie about our little boy's teeth and tail. We didn't think she'd agree to stay on and we didn't want our secret to get out.

We were in our bathroom when he was born. I bought an extra large tub just for the occasion. Shannon had a play list of songs she wanted played on repeat. We had a bunch of candles all around the room, and the birth-plan called for me to 'catch' the baby.

Elsie showed up and did her thing. To our surprise, it was time for Shannon to push within twenty minutes of our birthing coach's arrival.

I'm not a man who gets flustered too easily. But if I was ever gonna vomit from nervousness, my son's birth would have been that time. After just a half hour of pushing it became obvious to Elsie that Shannon was having an inordinate amount of trouble pushing. She was nearly unconscious after every push, and it wasn't getting any easier. Me catching the baby was out of the question. After an hour Elsie was ready to call an ambulance, she said it was her duty to ensure the health and safety of the baby through any complications.

I snatched the cell phone out of Elsie's hand, which may not have been necessary based on Shannon's screams of protest. I wouldn't have disobeyed a woman in that much agony.

After another terrifying hour, she was crowning. I remember when I had my first apartment that I wanted a dog, and picked out the most pathetic creature the pound had to offer. That dog's wet and neglected fur looked just like the hair on the top of my son's head.

After the rest of the baby's head came out, Elsie pulled back in panic. I threatened her until she got back in there and delivered my son. With tears flowing from her shiny brown eyes, she agreed.

With every centimeter of my little boy that came out of Shannon, I could feel Elsie's aura of disgust growing in intensity. Once his feet were clear, he started acting like what I always suspected he was. A rat.

He ate his umbilical cord. Not the whole thing, but he chomped it and I'd be willing to bet he swallowed it.

Elsie threw up. To be fair, she was under the impression that she was going through a standard home birth. Who would have expected to help birth a monster?

He responded to her disgust. Just ten seconds old and the eight pound rat lunged at Elsie. He went for the throat. But Dad was there to run interference. As he was jumping towards her I moved in to take the hit. What I actually did was push his trajectory lower.

I assume Elsie still has a pretty deep scar. He bit Elsie deep just above her left breast. Her loose fitting school bus yellow blouse became red immediately. I pulled him off and she ran away screaming. We never saw her again. I don't know how Muffy did it to this day, but Elsie never talked. Even though it took all my strength to restrain his attacks, I finally got to hold my little boy.

But now Andy has escaped. He's six years older and six years stronger than that fateful day he was born. I've woken up at night, terrified at the thought that my little boy would get out and hurt himself or someone else.

I keep my lawn immaculate. It may be a little overboard, but I mow the grass twice a week. It was easy to track his paw prints in the grass. I followed the scuffles in the perfect lines of my lawn for a hundred feet to the poorly-maintained street I live on. My nearest neighbors have a half mile buffer zone between us and them, so I knew Andy must be going to the next house.

If I wasn't feeling ill already, the half mile sprint to the neighbor's house made the suggestion of nausea in my stomach materialize as a fact. The fact that the front door was swinging open did nothing to ease my stomach either.

Apparently my neighbor was a lawn fanatic as well, because the unmistakable signature of my son's paws was apparent in the diagonal lines of the grass. Andy must have hurt himself chewing his way out of the attic, because there were miniscule bloodstains on the farmer's porch before the front door.

I walked up to the house, already knowing what I would find inside. For so many years I'd known it was just a matter of time until he got out. Every night when I couldn't sleep I'd see a different scenario over and over again in my head. It was like when I was a punk in my early twenties. I'd lost my license for some stupid failure to pay a fine. I didn't have the money to get it back, so I said screw it and just drove like it was fine. Every day I'd get behind the wheel and picture in my head what it would be like when I got pulled over.

Getting arrested, bailing myself out a couple of hours later, I'd even pictured going to the impound lot to get my car out. When I finally did get pulled over, and the cop was cuffing me, it was even more surreal since I'd pictured it so many times in my head. That's what it was like searching fro Andy; a dream I'd had a thousand times. But this wasn't going to be as simple as forty bucks bail and a court date.

My neighbors kept the gray carpet in their foyer as meticulously clean as their front lawn. It was easy to see Andy's claw marks in the rug.

Walking down the hallway towards what I assumed was the kitchen, I didn't have time to stop and look at the family photos on the wall. Not that I would have been able to recognize the faces I saw in the kitchen as the ones in the photos.

They must have been getting ready to eat, because I could smell something burning. A woman a few years older than Shannon was on the floor in an awkward position, her face pushed up against the bottom drawer of the oven with the rest of her body flat on the linoleum. The pool of blood seemed to be spreading out, and there was a trail on the door of the oven leading down to what I assumed to be a bloody mess of a face. Andy's red paw prints led to my left, towards a high-ceilinged living room.

All I had to do was follow the prints with my eyes and they landed on what I assumed to be the man of the house, looking much like his wife. That's when I heard the scratching upstairs.

I sprinted up the carpeted steps, only half noticing the gory track marks underfoot. At the top I turned right and saw him.

Andy was scratching at a door, making pretty good headway on a hole at the bottom. His fur had thinned out over the years, and his spine stuck out at a strange angle over his hunched back, like the seam on an imperfect pair of pants. He turned around and I could see some demented spark of recognition in his completely red eyes. He even opened his mouth slightly, and a small clump of meat fell off of one of the teeth that crowded out of his mouth. He turned towards me and lifted his claws. For a split second I thought he wanted to hug his daddy. But then the long pink tail swung around and hit the door, leaving a red slash below the door knob. It was reminiscent of my childhood. It was something I swore I'd never do, but I had no choice. When my son was in the air, already opening that hole of jagged teeth of a mouth and turning his face towards me for better access to my throat, I slugged him right in the side of the head.

He went down. My boy is strong, but what six-year-old can take a right hook from a fully grown man and come up swinging?

I quickly threw him in the bathroom next to me before he recovered.

At the time I assumed a child was cowering behind that door my son was clawing under. But when I opened the door, I realized cowering wasn't the right word for it, because I caught a wooden bat to the ribs.

"You're safe, kid! It's in the bathroom, knocked out! I'm here to help!" I yelled as I backed away holding my ribs.

"Is my Mum and Dad okay? I heard them screaming and then I went to check on them and that thing came after me," the boy said.

I didn't know what to say. I've done some stuff I'm not proud of, but I've been able to get past them and live my life as an adult with a clear conscience. But hearing this little kid, no older than my boy, ask about his parents' safety after nearly dying at the hands of a four foot tall rat, broke my heart. That was the moment I found out guilt was the worst feeling of all.

"They're fine, buddy. But I'm gonna have to take care of the monster. Can you go wait out front for me while I make sure the monster's really knocked out? I wouldn't want him to scare anybody else. Where does your dad keep the duct tape?" Every word was fake. I could barely contain my tears. The kid actually *smiled* when I said his parents were fine. I had no game plan, but I knew the next neighbors were about a half mile away, and I wasn't lying to another kid today.

He told me where his dad kept the duct tape. I walked through the house in a trance. Not the surreal feeling of before, not the feeling of recognition, but a new feeling, like I might have crossed the line from repentant petty criminal to full on Bad Guy. I couldn't get the kid's face out of my mind's eye.

I found the duct tape and went back to the upstairs bathroom. After putting my ear to the door to make sure I wasn't in for a surprise, I walked in and stood over my son's unconscious body.

The idea of murdering my son went through my head. I really considered doing it for about one second. Then I shook it off. I didn't want to be a Bad Guy.

I used the entire roll of tape to bind his hands and feet together. I even taped his tail to his body, leaving a small loop so I could drag him. This part, believe it or not, I had pictured before. The little boy was waiting for me on the front lawn. I told him his phone wasn't working and that we'd have to go back to my house to call the police. I told him his parents were fixing the door and they'd come get him in a little bit. He accepted every word of it.

I dragged my son behind me the entire half mile back to my house. Shannon was waiting on the front porch. The look of relief when she saw us only lasted as long as it took to register the boy's presence. She figured it out right away.

The rest of the day was a merciful blur. After chaining Andy up more securely, Shannon and I continued our lies to the new orphan. I destroyed the evidence of Andy's killings at the neighbors in a fiery blaze. The quick motions and half-thought-out actions of the last few hours only came to a halt when I returned home. The boy was sitting in our living room eating ice cream, apparently sold on the fact that his parents were busy but would be coming for him soon.

"Now what?" Shannon asked.

It was a question I'd half considered at best. There were so many options, but they all lead to me being the Bad Guy. I'd been bad enough for one day. There was only one course of action. Only one thing I could do to stay a good father and keep myself from falling apart with guilt.

I looked at Shannon with a slight grin and said, "I've always been of the opinion that our son should have a brother..."

THE BURIAL OF THE RATS

BRAM STOKER

Leaving Paris by the Orleans road, cross the Enceinte, and turning to the right, you find yourself in a somewhat wild and not at all savory district. Right and left, before and behind, on every side rise great mounds of debris and waste accumulated by the process of time.

Paris has its night as well as its day life, and the sojourner who enters his hotel in the Rue de Rivoli or the Rue St. Honore late at night or leaves it early in the morning, can guess in coming near Montrouge—if he hasn't done so already—the purpose of those great wagons that look like boilers on wheels which can be seen everywhere.

Every city has its peculiar institutions created out of its own needs, and one of the most notable institutions of Paris is its rag-picking population.

In the early morning—and Parisian life commences at an early hour—may be seen in most streets standing on the pathway opposite every court and alley and between every few houses, as still in some American cities, even in parts of New York, large wooden boxes into which the domestics or tenement-holders empty the accumulated waste of the past day.

Around these boxes gather squalid, hungry-looking men and women, the implements of whose craft consists of a coarse bag or basket slung over their shoulders, and a little rake with which they turn over and probe and examine in the minutest manner the trash. They pick up and deposit in their baskets, by aid of their rakes, whatever they may find, with the same facility as a Chinaman uses his chopsticks.

Paris is a city of centralization—and centralization and classification are closely allied. In the early times, when centralization was becoming a fact, its forerunner was classification. All things which are similar or analogous become grouped together, and from the grouping of groups rises one whole or central point. We see radiating many long arms with innumerable tentacles, and in the center a gigantic head with a comprehensive brain, keen eyes to look on every side, ears sensitive to hear, and a voracious mouth to swallow.

Other cities resemble all the birds and beasts and fishes whose appetites and digestions are normal. Paris alone is the analogical apotheosis of the octopus. Product of centralization carried to an ad absurdum, it fairly represents the devil fish, and in no respects is the resemblance more curious than in the similarity of the digestive apparatus.

Those intelligent tourists who 'do' Paris in three days, are often puzzled to know how it is that the dinner which in London would cost about six shillings can be had for three francs in a cafe in the Palais Royal. They need have no more wonder if they will but consider the classification which is a theoretic specialty of Parisian life, and adopt the fact from which the chiffonier has his genesis.

The Paris of 1850 wasn't like the Paris of today, and those who see the Paris of Napoleon and Baron Hausseman can hardly realize the existence of the state of things forty-five years ago.

Amongst other things, however, which haven't changed, are those districts where the waste is gathered. Trash is trash all the world over, in every age, and the family likeness of trash piles is perfect. The traveler, therefore, who visits the environs of Montrouge can go back easily and without difficulty to the year 1850.

In this year I was making a prolonged stay in Paris. I was very much in love with a young lady who, though she returned my passion, so far had yielded to the wishes of her parents that she'd promised not to see me or to correspond with me for a year. I, too, had been compelled to accede to these conditions under a vague hope of parental approval. During the term of probation I'd promised to remain out of the country and not to write to my dear one until the expiration of the year.

Naturally the time went heavily with me. There was no one of my own family or friends who could tell me of Alice, and none of her relatives had, I'm sorry to say, sufficient generosity to send me even an occasional word of comfort regarding her health and well-being.

I spent six months wandering about Europe, but as I could find no satisfactory distraction in travel, I determined to come to Paris, where at least I'd be within easy reach of London in case any good fortune should call me there before the appointed time. That 'hope deferred makes the heart sick' was never better exemplified than in my case, for in addition to the perpetual longing to see the face of the woman I loved, there was always with me a harrowing anxiety lest some accident should prevent me showing Alice in due time that I had, throughout the long period of probation, been faithful to her trust and my own love. Thus, every adventure which I undertook had a fierce pleasure of its own, for it was fraught with possible consequences greater than it would have ordinarily borne

Like all travelers I exhausted the places of most interest in the first month of my stay, and was driven in the second month to look for amusement wherever I might find it. Having made sundry journeys to the better-known suburbs, I began to see that there was a terra incognita, in so far as the guide book was concerned, in the social wilderness lying between these attractive points. Accordingly I began to systematize my researches, and each day took up the thread of my exploration at the place where I had on the previous day dropped it.

In the process of time my wanderings led me near Montrouge, and I saw that hereabouts lay the epitome of social exploration—a country as little known as that one around the source of the White Nile. I determined to investigate philosophically the chiffonier: his habitat, life, and his means of life.

The job was an unsavory one and difficult to accomplish, with little hope of adequate reward. However, despite reason, obstinacy prevailed, and I entered into my new investigation with a keener energy than I could have summoned to aid me in any investigation leading to any end, either valuable or worthy.

One day, late on a fine afternoon and near the end of September, I entered the holy of holies of the city of trash. The place was evidently the recognized abode of a number of chiffoniers, for some sort of arrangement was manifested in the formation of the trash piles near the road. I passed amongst these mounds, which stood like orderly sentries, determined to penetrate further and trace the trash to its ultimate location.

As I passed along I saw behind the mound a few small forms that flitted back and forth, evidently watching with interest the advent of any stranger to such a place. The district was like a small Switzerland, and as I went forward, my tortuous course shut out the path behind me.

Presently I came to what seemed like a small city or community of wooden dressers and cabinets. There were a number of shanties or huts, such as may be met with in the remote parts of the Bog of Allan, rude places with wattled walls, plastered with mud and roofs of thatch made from stable refuse. Such places that you wouldn't want to enter for any consideration, and which even in water-color could only look picturesque if judiciously treated.

In the midst of these huts was one of the strangest adaptations—I can't say habitations—I'd ever seen. An immense old wardrobe, the colossal remnant of some boudoir of Charles VII or

Henry II, had been converted into a dwelling-house. The double doors lay open, so that the entire structure was open to public view.

In the open half of the wardrobe was a common sitting-room of some four feet by six, in which sat, smoking their pipes around a charcoal brazier, no fewer than six old soldiers of the First Republic, with their uniforms torn and worn.

Evidently they were of the *mauvais sujet* class; their bleary eyes and limp jaws told plainly of a common love of absinthe, and their eyes had that haggard, worn look of slumbering ferocity which follows hard in the wake of heavy drinking.

The other side still had its shelves intact, save that they were cut to half their depth, and on each shelf there was a bed made of rags and straw. The half-dozen residents that inhabited this structure looked at me curiously as I passed, and when I looked back after going a little way I saw their heads close together in a whispered conference.

I didn't like the look of it at all, for the place was very empty of life, and the men looked very, very villainous. But I didn't see any cause for fear and went on my way, penetrating further and further into the area. The way was tortuous to a degree, and from going around in a series of semi-circles, I grew rather confused with regard to the points of the compass.

When I'd penetrated a little way I saw, as I turned the corner of a small pile, sitting on a mound of straw, an old soldier wearing a threadbare coat.

"Hello!" I said to myself, "the First Republic is represented well here in its soldiery."

As I passed him, the old man never even looked up at me, but gazed at the ground with stolid persistency. Again I remarked to myself, "See what a life of rude warfare can do! This old man's curiosity is a thing of the past."

But when I had gone a few steps, I looked back suddenly and saw that curiosity wasn't dead, for the veteran had raised his head and was regarding me with a very odd expression. He seemed to look a lot like one of the six soldiers I'd seen before. When he saw me looking, he dropped his head, and without thinking further of him I went on my way, satisfied that there was a strange likeness between these old warriors.

Presently I met another old soldier in a similar manner. He, too, did not notice me as I passed him. By this time it was getting late in the afternoon, and I began to think of retracing my steps. Accordingly, I turned to go back, but could see a number of tracks leading between different mounds and couldn't ascertain which of them I should take. In my perplexity I wanted to see someone who I could ask the way, but there was no one to see. I determined to go on a few mounds further and try to see someone—but not a veteran.

I gained my object, for after going a couple of hundred yards I saw before me a single shanty such as I'd seen before, with the difference being that this wasn't a structure for living in, but merely a roof with three walls, and open in front. From the evidences which the neighborhood exhibited, I took it to be a place for sorting. Within it was an old woman, wrinkled and bent with age. I approached her to ask the way.

She rose as I came close and I asked her my question. She immediately commenced a conversation, and it occurred to me that here in the very center of the Kingdom of Trash was the place to gather details of the history of Parisian rag-picking, particularly as I could now do so from the lips of one who looked like the oldest inhabitant.

I began my inquiries, and the old woman gave me most interesting answers. She'd been one of the people who sat daily before the guillotine and had taken an active part among the women who signalized themselves by their violence in the revolution.

While we were talking, she said suddenly, "But m'sieur must be tired standing," and dusted off a rickety old stool for me to sit on. I didn't want to do so for many reasons, but the poor old woman was so civil that I didn't want to run the risk of hurting her by refusing, and moreover the conversation of one who'd been at the taking of the Bastille was so interesting that I sat down.

While we were talking an old man— he was older and more bent and wrinkled than the woman—appeared from behind the shanty.

"Here is Pierre," she said. "M'sieur can hear stories now if he wishes, for Pierre was in everything, from the Bastille to Waterloo."

The old man took another stool at my request and we plunged into a sea of revolutionary reminiscences. This old man, albeit clothed like a scarecrow, was like any one of the six veterans.

I was now sitting in the center of the low hut with the woman on my left and the man on my right, each of them being somewhat in front of me. The place was full of all sorts of curious objects of lumber, and of many more things that I wished weren't. In one corner was a pile of rags which seemed to move from the number of vermin it contained, and in the other a pile of bones with an odor that was rather potent. Every now and then, glancing at the piles, I could see the gleaming eyes of some of the rats which infested the place. These loathsome creatures were bad enough, but what looked even more dreadful was an old butcher's axe with an iron handle. Leaning up against the wall on the right hand side, it was stained with clots of blood. Still, these things didn't give me much concern. The talk of the two old people was so fascinating that I stayed for a while, until the evening came and the trash mounds threw dark shadows over the vales between them.

After a time I began to grow uneasy. I couldn't tell why, but somehow I didn't feel satisfied. Uneasiness is an instinct and a means of warning. The psychic faculties are often the sentries of the intellect, and when they sound the alarm the reason begins to act, although perhaps not consciously.

This was so with me. I began to rethink me where I was and what surrounded me, and to wonder how I would fare in case I was attacked. Then the thought suddenly burst upon me, although without any overt cause, that I was in danger. Prudence whispered: "Be still and make no sign." So I was still and made no sign, for I knew that four cunning eyes were on me. Four eyes if not more. My God, what a horrible thought! The shanty might be surrounded on three sides with killers! I might be in the midst of a band of such cutthroats as only half a century of periodic revolution can produce.

With a sense of danger filling me up, my intellect and observation quickened, and I grew more watchful. I noticed that the old woman's eyes were constantly wandering towards my hands. I looked at them, too, and saw the cause—my rings. On my left little finger I had a large signet and on the right a good size diamond.

I thought that if there was any danger then my first care was to avert suspicion. Accordingly, I began to work the conversation around to rag-picking and of the things found there, and so by easy stages to jewels. Then, seizing a favorable opportunity, I asked the old woman if she knew anything of such things. She answered that she did, a little. I held out my right hand, and showing her the diamond, asked her what she thought of it. She answered that her eyes were bad, and stooped over my hand.

I said as nonchalantly as I could, "Pardon me. You'll see better this way!" Then taking it off, I handed it to her. An unholy light came into her withered old face when she touched it. She stole one glance at me swift and keen as a flash of lightning.

She bent over the ring for a moment, her face concealed, as though she was examining the ring. The old man looked straight out of the front of the shanty before him, at the same time fumbling in his pockets and producing a wad of tobacco wrapped in paper and a pipe, which he proceeded to fill.

I took advantage of the pause and the momentary rest from the searching eyes on my face to look carefully around the place, now dim and shadowy in the gloom. There were still piles of varied reeking foulness, and the chilling blood-stained axe leaning against the wall in the corner, and everywhere, despite the gloom, the baleful glitter of the eyes of the rats. I could see them even through some of the chinks of the boards at the back, down close to the ground. But then I realized that these eyes seemed more than usually large and bright and baleful.

For an instant my heart stood still, and I felt in that whirling condition of mind in which one feels a sort of spiritual drunkenness, as though the body is only maintained erect because there is no time for it to fall before recovery. Then, in another second, I was calm—coldly calm—with all my energies in full vigor, with a self-control which I felt to be perfect, with all my instincts on full alert.

Now I knew the full extent of my danger. I was watched and surrounded by desperate people! I couldn't even guess at how many of them were lying there on the ground behind the shanty, waiting for the moment to strike. I knew that I was big and strong, and they knew it, too. They also knew, as I did, that I was an Englishman and would put up a fight. So we waited.

I felt that I'd gained an advantage in the last few seconds, for I knew my danger and understood the situation. Now, I thought, is the test of my courage—the enduring test. The fighting test might come later.

The old woman raised her head and said to me in a satisfied kind of way, "A very fine ring, indeed, a beautiful ring! Oh, my! I once had such rings, plenty of them, and bracelets and earrings! Oh, for in those fine days I led the town a dance! But they've forgotten me now! They've forgotten me! They? Why, they never heard of me! Perhaps their grandfathers remember me, some of them!" She laughed a harsh, croaking laugh. Then I'm bound to say that she astonished me, for she handed me back the ring with a certain suggestion of old-fashioned grace which wasn't without its pathos.

The old man eyed her with a sort of sudden ferocity, half rising from his stool, and said to me suddenly and hoarsely, "Let me see!"

I was about to hand the ring over when the old woman said, "No! No, don't give it to Pierre! Pierre is eccentric. He loses things, and such a pretty ring it is!"

"Cat!" the old man said savagely.

Suddenly, the old woman said, rather more loudly than was necessary, "Wait! I shall tell you something about a ring."

There was something in the sound of her voice that jarred upon me. Perhaps it was my hyper-sensitiveness, wound up as I was to such a pitch of nervous excitement, but I seemed to think that she wasn't addressing me. As I stole a glance around the place, I saw the eyes of the rats in the bone pile, but missed the eyes along the back wall. But even as I looked I saw them again appear. The old woman's "Wait!" had given me a respite from attack, and the men had sunk back to their reclining posture.

"I once lost a ring, a beautiful diamond hoop that had belonged to a queen, and which was given to me by a farmer of the taxes, who afterwards cut his throat because I sent him away. I thought it must have been stolen, and taxed my people, but I could get no trace. The police came and suggested that it had found its way to the drain. We descended. I was in my fine clothes, for I wouldn't trust them with my beautiful ring. I know more of the drains since then, and of rats, too! But I'll never forget the horror of that place. It was alive with blazing eyes, a wall of them just outside the light of our torches. Well, we got beneath my house. We searched the outlet of the drain, and there in the filth found my ring. Then we came out.

"But we found something else, too! As we were coming toward the opening, a lot of sewer rats—human ones this time—came towards us. They told the police that one of their number had gone into the drain, but hadn't returned. He'd gone in only shortly before we had, and if lost, could hardly be far off. They asked help to seek him, so we turned back. They tried to prevent me going, but I insisted. It was exciting. We didn't go far until we came on something. There was only a little water, and the bottom of the drain was raised with brick, rubbish and the like when we found him. He'd made a fight for it, even when his torch had gone out. But they were too many for him to win! They'd not been long about it, too! The bones were still warm, but they'd been picked clean. They'd even eaten their own dead ones, as there were bones of rats as well as of the man. They took it cool enough those others—-the human ones—-and joked of their comrade when they found him dead, though they would have helped him if he'd been still living. Bah, what matters it—life or death?"

"Weren't you scared?" I asked her.

"Scared!" she said with a laugh. "Me? Ask Pierre! But I was younger then, and as I came through that horrible drain with its wall of greedy eyes, always moving with the circle of the light from the torches, I didn't feel easy. I kept on before the men, though! It's a way I have! I never let the men get it before me. All I want is a chance and a means! And they ate him up—took every trace away except the bones, and no one knew it, nor no sound of him was ever heard!"

Here she broke into a chuckling fit of the ghastliest merriment which it was ever my lot to hear and see. A great poetess describes her heroine singing: "Oh, to see or hear her singing! Scarce I know which is the divinest."

I can apply the same idea to the old crone, in all save the divinity, for I could scarcely tell which was the most hellish—the harsh, malicious, satisfied, cruel laugh, the leering grin, the horrible square opening of the mouth like a tragic mask, or the yellow gleam of the few discolored teeth in the shapeless gums. In that laugh, grin and the chuckling, the satisfaction I knew as well as if it had been spoken to me in words of thunder that my murder was settled, and the murderers only bided the proper time for its accomplishment. I could read between the lines of her gruesome story the commands to her accomplices. "Wait," she seemed to say, "bide your time. I will strike the first blow. Find the weapon for me, and I'll make the opportunity! He won't escape! Keep him quiet, and then no one will be wiser. There'll be no outcry, and the rats will do their work!"

It was growing darker and darker; the night was coming. I stole a glance around the shanty; it was still the same: the bloody axe in the corner, the mounds of filth, the eyes in the bone pile, and in the crannies of the floor.

Pierre had been still ostensibly filling his pipe, and he now struck a light and began to puff away at it.

The old woman said, "Dear heart, how dark it is! Pierre, light the lamp like a good lad!"

Pierre got up, and with the lighted match in his hand, touched the wick of a lamp which hung at one side of the entrance to the shanty; it had a reflector that threw the light all over the place. It was evidently that which was used for their sorting at night.

"Not that, stupid! Not that! The lantern!" she called out to him.

He immediately blew it out, saying, "All right, mother I'll find it." Then he hustled about the left corner of the room.

The old woman said through the darkness, "The lantern! The lantern! Oh! That's the light that's most useful to us poor folks. The lantern was the friend of the revolution! It's the friend of the people! It helps us when all else fails."

Hardly had she said this when there was a kind of creaking of the whole place, and something was steadily dragged over the roof. Again I seemed to read between the lines of her words. I knew the lesson of the lantern.

"One of you get on the roof with a noose and strangle him as he passes out if we fail within."

As I looked out of the opening, I saw the loop of a rope outlined black against the lurid sky. I was now, indeed, beset! Pierre wasn't long in finding the lantern. I kept my eyes fixed through the darkness on the old woman. Pierre struck his light, and by its flash I saw the old woman raise a long sharp knife or dagger from the ground beside her where it had been, then hide it in the folds of her gown. It seemed to be like a butcher's sharpening iron honed to a keen point.

The lantern was lit.

"Bring it here, Pierre," she said. "Place it in the doorway where we can see it. See how nice it is! It shuts out the darkness from us; it's just right!"

Just right for her and her purposes! It threw all its light on my face, leaving in gloom the faces of both Pierre and the old woman, who sat on each side of me and just in front.

I felt that the time of action was approaching, but I knew now that the first signal and movement would come from the old woman, so I watched her carefully. I was all unarmed, but I'd made up my mind what to do. At her first movement I'd seize the butcher's axe in the corner and fight my way out. I would make them work for their kill. I stole a glance around to fix the axe's exact location so that I couldn't fail to seize it at the first effort, for then, if ever, time and accuracy would be precious.

But when I looked for it I found it was gone! All the horror of the situation burst upon me, but the bitterest thought of all was that if the issue of the terrible position should be against me, Alice would infallibly suffer. Either she would believe me false—and any lover, or anyone who has ever been one, can imagine the bitterness of the thought—or else she would go on loving long after I'd been lost to her and the world, so that her life would be broken and embittered, shattered with disappointment and despair.

The very magnitude of the pain braced me up and nerved me to bear the dread scrutiny of the plotters. I think I didn't betray myself. The old woman was watching me as a cat does a mouse. She had her right hand hidden in the folds of her gown, clutching, I knew, that long, cruel-looking dagger. Had she seen any disappointment in my face she would, I felt, have known that the moment had come, and would have sprung on me like a tigress, certain of taking me unprepared.

I looked out into the night, and there I saw new cause for danger. Before and around the hut were at a little distance some shadowy forms. They were quite still, but I knew that they were all alert and on guard. Small chance for me now in that direction.

Again I stole a glance around the place. In moments of great excitement and danger, the mind works very quickly, and the keenness of the faculties which depend on the mind grows in proportion. I now felt this. In an instant I took in the entire situation. I saw that the axe had been taken through a small hole made in one of the rotten boards. How rotten they must be to allow such a thing to be done without any noise.

The hut was a regular murder-trap, and was guarded all around. A garroter lay on the roof, ready to entangle me with his noose if I should escape the dagger of the old hag. In front the way was guarded by I know not how many watchers. And at the back was a row of desperate men. I still saw their eyes through the crack in the boards of the floor when last I looked, as they lay prone, waiting for the signal to act. If it was ever to be, the time was now.

As nonchalantly as I could, I turned slightly on my stool so as to get my right leg well under me. Then with a sudden jump, turning my head and guarding it with my hands, and with the fighting instinct of the knights of old, I breathed my lady's name, and hurled myself against the back wall of the hut.

Watchful as they were, the suddenness of my movement surprised both Pierre and the old woman. As I crashed through the rotten timbers, I saw the old woman rise up with a leap like a tiger and heard her low gasp of baffled rage. My feet slid on something that moved, and as I jumped away I knew that I'd stepped on the back of one of the men lying on their faces outside the hut. I was torn with nails and splinters as I burst through the wall, but was otherwise unhurt. Breathless, I rushed up the trash mound in front of me, hearing as I went the dull crash of the shanty as it collapsed into a mass of debris.

It was a nightmare climb. The mound, though low, was awfully steep, and with each step I took the mass of dust and cinders tore down with me and gave way under my feet. The dust rose up and choked me; it was a sickening, fetid, awful climb, but climb I did, and either for life or death, I struggled on. The seconds seemed like hours, but the few moments lead I had, combined with my youth and strength, gave me a great advantage, and though several forms struggled after me in deadly silence—which was more dreadful than any sound—I easily reached the top.

Since then I've climbed the cone of Vesuvius, and as I struggled up that dreary mound amid the sulfurous fumes, the memory of that awful night at Montrouge came flooding back to me so vividly that I almost grew faint.

The mound was one of the tallest in the region of trash, and as I struggled to the top, panting for breath and with my heart beating like a sledgehammer, I saw to my left the dull red gleam of the sky, and nearer still the flashing of lights. Thank God! I knew where I was now and where lay the road to Paris!

For two or three seconds I paused and looked back. My pursuers were still behind me, but struggling up resolutely, and in deadly silence. Beyond, the shanty was a wreck, nothing but a mass of broken timber and moving forms. I could see it well, for flames were already bursting out. The rags and straw had evidently caught fire from the lantern. Still there was silence there. Not a sound. Those old wretches could die quietly, anyhow.

I had no time for more than a passing glance, for as I cast an eye around the mound, preparing to make my descent, I saw several dark forms rushing around on either side to cut me off. It was now a race for life. They were trying to head me off on my way to Paris; with the instinct of the moment I dashed down to the right-hand side. I was just in time, too, for though I went down the mound in a few steps, the wary old men who were watching me turned back, and as I rushed by into the opening between the two mounds in front, one of them almost struck me a blow with that terrible butcher's axe. There could surely not be two such weapons lying about!

Then began a really horrible chase. I easily ran ahead of the old men, and even when some younger ones and a few women joined in the hunt, I easily outdistanced them. But I didn't know the way, and I couldn't even guide myself by the light in the sky, for I was running away from it. I'd heard that, unless of conscious purpose, hunted men always turned to the left, and so I found it now, and so I suppose, did my pursuers, who were more animals than men, and with either cunning or instinct had found out such secrets for themselves. For on finishing a quick spurt, after which I intended to take a moment to catch my breath, I suddenly saw ahead of me two or three forms swiftly passing behind a mound to the right.

I was in the spider's web now indeed! But with the thought of this new danger came the resource of the hunted, and I darted down the next turning to the right. I continued in this direction for some hundred yards, then made a turn to the left again, feeling certain that I'd avoided the danger of being surrounded.

But the rabble was still following me: steady, dogged, relentless, and still in grim silence. In the greater darkness the mounds seemed now to be somewhat smaller than before, although they looked bigger in proportion. I was now well ahead of my pursuers, so I made a dart up the mound in front of me.

I was close to the edge of this inferno of trash mounds. Behind me the red light of Paris was in the sky, and towering up behind rose the heights of Montmarte—a dim light, with here and there brilliant points like stars.

Restored to vigor in a moment, I ran over the few remaining mounds of decreasing size, and found myself on the level land that lay beyond. Even then, however, the prospect wasn't inviting, for before me was dark and dismal, and I'd evidently come on one of those dank, low-lying waste places which are found here and there in the neighborhood of great cities. Places of waste and desolation, where the space is required for the ultimate agglomeration of all that is noxious, and the ground is so contaminated as to create no desire of occupancy even in the lowest squatter.

With eyes accustomed to the gloom of the evening, and away now from the shadows of those dreadful trash mounds, I could see much more easily than I could a little while ago. It might have been, of course, that the glare in the sky of the lights of Paris, though the city was some miles away, was reflected here. But whatever it was, I saw well enough to get my bearings.

In front of me was a bleak, flat waste that seemed almost dead level with the dark shimmering pools of stagnant water. Seemingly far off on the right, amid a small cluster of scattered lights, rose the dark mass of Fort Montrouge, and away to the left in the distance, pointed with stray gleams from cottage windows, the lights in the sky showed the location of Bicetre. After a moment's thought I decided to go to the right and try to reach Montrouge. There at least would be some sort of safety, and I might possibly before long come upon some of the crossroads which I knew.

Somewhere, not far off, must be the strategic road that connected the outlying chain of forts circling the city. Then I looked back. Coming over the mounds and outlined black against the glare of the Parisian horizon, I saw several moving figures, and to the right several more forms deploying out between me and my destination. They evidently meant to cut me off in this direction, and so my choice became constricted; it lay now between going straight ahead or turning to the left.

Stooping to the ground, so as to get the advantage of the horizon as a line of sight, I looked carefully in this direction, but could detect no sign of my enemies. I figured that since they'd not guarded or were not trying to guard that point, there was evidently danger there for me already. So I made up my mind to go straight ahead.

It wasn't an inviting prospect, and as I went on, the reality grew worse. The ground became soft and squishy, and now and again gave out beneath me in a sickening kind of way. I seemed somehow to be going down, for I saw around me places seemingly more elevated than where I was, and this in a place which from a little way back seemed dead level.

I searched behind me, but could see none of my pursuers. This was strange, for all along these vagabonds had followed me through the darkness as if it was broad daylight. How I blamed myself for coming out in my light-colored tourist suit of tweed. The silence, and my not being able to see my enemies, though I felt that they were watching me, grew appalling. In the hope of someone not of the ghastly crew hearing me, I raised my voice and shouted several times. There wasn't the slightest response; not even an echo rewarded my efforts. For a while I stood stock still and kept my eyes in one direction. On one of the rising places around me I saw something dark move along, then another, and another. This was to my left, and it was seemingly moving to head me off.

With my skill as a runner, I thought that I might again elude my enemies at this game of cat and mouse, and so with all my speed I darted forward.

In a wet splash my feet gave way into a mass of slimy rubbish, and I fell headlong into a reeking, stagnant pool. The water and the mud in which my arms sank up to the elbows was filthy and nauseous beyond description, and in the suddenness of my fall I actually swallowed some of the filthy liquid, which nearly choked me and made me gasp for breath.

As I looked up, I found a hundred eyes surrounding me, and I knew instantly that the rats had come out of hiding, thinking that their meal was at hand. They surrounded me, their whiskers twitching, the incisors flaring in the night. I could see they were about to pounce, to swarm over me, so I grabbed the first thing I could find, a thick piece of wood, and I used it as a club, smacking the foul beasts from me again and again. Seeing that their meal wasn't dead yet, wasn't as helpless as they might have hoped, the foul rodents hissed and squealed before running off into the night. But though they left, a second later I saw the eyes upon me, only now from a further distance. It appeared they were willing to bide their time and wait until I was totally helpless.

I'll never forget the moments during which I stood trying to recover, almost fainting from the fetid odor of the filthy pool—a white mist rose ghostlike around it. Worst of all, with the acute despair of the hunted animal when he sees the pursuing pack closing in on him, I saw before my eyes while I stood helpless, the dark forms of my pursuers moving swiftly to surround me.

It's curious how our minds work on odd matters even when the energies of thought are seemingly concentrated on some terrible and pressing need. I was in momentary peril of my life: my safety depended on my action, and my choice of alternatives coming now with almost every step I took, and yet I couldn't help but think of the strange and dogged persistency of these old men.

Their silent resolution, their steadfast, grim persistency even in such a cause commanded, as well as fear, even a measure of respect. I wondered what they must have been like in the vigor of their youth. I could understand now that whirlwind rush on the bridge of Arcola, that scornful exclamation of the Old Guard at Waterloo. Ruminations has its own pleasures, even at such moments, but fortunately it doesn't in any way clash with the thought from which action springs.

I realized at a glance that so far I was defeated in my goal; my enemies had won. They'd succeeded in surrounding me on three sides, and were bent on driving me off to the left, where there was already some danger for me, for they had left no guard. I accepted the alternative—it was a case of running. I had to keep low to the ground, for my pursuers were on the higher places, but the ooze and broken ground impeded me.

My youth and training made me able to hold my ground, and by keeping a diagonal line I not only kept them from gaining on me, but I even began to outdistance them. This gave me new hope and strength, and by this time habitual training was beginning to tell and my second wind had come.

Before me the land rose slightly. I rushed up the slope and found before me a waste of watery slime, with a low dike or bank that looked black and grim. I felt that if I could reach that dike, there would be safety there. With solid ground under my feet and some kind of path to guide me, I could find with comparative ease a way out of my troubles. After a glance right and left and seeing no one near, I focused my attention for few minutes on watching where I put my feet while I crossed the swamp. It was rough going, hard work, but there was little danger, merely toil, and in a short time I arrived at the dike.

I rushed up the slope exulting, but here again I met a new shock. On either side of me rose a number of crouching figures. They rushed me from both sides. Each of them held a section of one large rope. The cordon was nearly complete. I couldn't pass on either side; the end was near.

There was only one chance and I took it. I hurled myself across the dike, escaping the very clutches of my foes as I threw myself into the stream. At any other time I would have thought the water foul and filthy, but now it was as welcome as the most crystal stream to a parched traveler. It was a highway of safety!

My pursuers rushed after me. Had only one of them held the rope it would have been all over for me, for he could have entangled me before I'd time to swim a stroke, but the many hands holding it delayed them, and when the rope struck the water, I heard the splash far behind me. A few minutes' hard swimming took me across the stream. Refreshed with the immersion and encouraged by the escape, I climbed the dike in comparatively good spirits.

From the top of the dike I looked back. Through the darkness I saw my assailants scattering up and down along the dike. The pursuit was evidently not ended, and again I had to choose my course. Beyond the dike where I stood was a wild, swampy space very similar to that which I'd crossed. I determined to shun such a place, and thought for a moment whether I would go up or down the dike. I thought I heard a sound—the muffled sound of oars—so I listened, then shouted out.

I received no response, but the sound ceased. My enemies had evidently found a boat of some kind. As they were on the up-side of me I took the down-path and began to run. As I passed to the left of where I'd entered the water, I heard several splashes, soft and stealthy, like the sound a rat makes as it plunges into the stream, but vastly greater. As I looked, I saw the dark sheen of the water broken by the ripples of several advancing human heads. Some of my enemies were swimming the stream also.

Behind me, up the stream, the silence was broken by the quick rattle and creak of oars; my enemies were in hot pursuit. I put my best leg foreword and ran on. After a couple of minutes, I looked back, and by a gleam of light through the clouds I saw several dark forms climbing the bank behind me.

The wind began to rise, and the water beside me was ruffled and beginning to break in tiny waves on the bank. I had to keep my eyes focused on the ground before me, lest I should stumble, for I knew that to trip was death. After a few minutes I looked back behind me.

On the dike were only a few dark figures, but crossing the swampy ground were many more. What new danger this portended I didn't know and could only guess. As I ran it seemed to me that my path kept ever sloping away to the right.

I looked up ahead and saw that the river was much wider than before, and that the dike on which I stood stretched for a good bit, and beyond it was another stream on whose near bank I saw some of the dark forms now across the marsh. I was on an island of some kind.

My situation was now indeed terrible, for my enemies had hemmed me in on every side. Behind came the quickening roll of the oars, as though my pursuers knew that the end was close. Around me on every side was desolation; there wasn't a roof or light as far as I could see.

Far off to the right rose some dark mass, but what it was I knew not. For a moment I paused to think what I should do, but just for a second, as my pursuers were drawing closer. Then my mind was made up. I slipped down the bank and took to the water. I struck out straight ahead so as to gain the current by clearing the backwater of the island, for such I presume it was, when I'd passed into the stream. I waited until a cloud moved across the moon to leave everything in darkness, then I took off my hat and laid it softly on the water to float with the stream, and a second after dived to the right and struck out under water with all my might.

I was about half a minute under water, and when I rose I came up as softly as I could, and turning, looked back. There went my light brown hat floating merrily away. Close behind my hat came a rickety old boat, driven furiously by a pair of oars. The moon was still partly obscured by the drifting clouds, but in the partial light I could see a man in the bow holding aloft and ready to strike what appeared to be that same dreadful pole-axe which I'd escaped before. As I looked the boat drew closer, and the man struck savagely at my hat.

The hat disappeared and the man fell forward, almost out of the boat. His comrades dragged him in but without the axe, and then as I turned with all my strength, bent on reaching the further bank, I heard the fierce hiss of a muttered, "Sacre!" which marked the anger of my baffled pursuers.

That was the first sound I'd heard from human lips during the whole dreadful chase, and full as it was with menace and danger to me, it was a welcome sound for it broke the awful silence that shrouded and appalled me. It was an overt sign that my opponents were men and not ghosts, and that with them I had, at least, the chance of a man, though but one against many.

But now that the spell of silence was broken, the sounds came thick and fast. From boat to shore and back from shore to boat came quick questions and answers, all in the fiercest whispers. I looked back—which was a fatal thing to do—for in that instant someone caught sight of my face, which showed white on the dark water, and shouted. Hands pointed to me and in a moment or two the boat was following hard after me. I'd but a little way to go, but quicker and quicker came the boat after me. I knew a few more strokes and I'd be on the shore, but I felt the coming of the boat, and expected each second to feel the crash of an oar or other weapon on my head. Had I not seen that dreadful axe disappear in the water, I don't think that I could have reached the shore. I heard the muttered curses of those not rowing and the labored breath of the rowers. With one supreme effort for life, I touched the bank and sprang up it. There wasn't a single second to spare, for right behind me the boat grounded on the bank and several dark forms sprang after me. I gained the top of the dike, and keeping to the left ran on again. The boat put off and followed down the stream.

Seeing this I feared danger in this direction, and quickly turning, ran down the dike on the other side, and after passing a short stretch of marshy ground, I gained a wild-open, flat country and sped on.

Still behind me came my relentless pursuers. Far away, below me, I saw the same dark mass as before, but now even closer. My heart gave a great thrill of delight, for I knew that it must be the fortress of Bicetre, and with new courage I ran on. I had heard that between each and all of the protecting forts of Paris there are strategic ways, deep sunk roads where soldiers marching could be sheltered from an enemy. I knew that if I could gain this road I'd be safe, but in the darkness I couldn't see any sign of it, so in blind hope of striking it, I ran on.

Presently I came to the edge of a deep cut in the earth, and found that down below me ran a road guarded on each side by a ditch of water fenced on either side by a straight, high wall. Getting fainter and dizzier, I ran on; the ground became more broken until I staggered and fell, and rose again, and ran on in the blind anguish of the hunted. Again the thought of Alice nerved me. I wouldn't be lost and wreck her life. I would fight and struggle for life to the bitter end.

With a great effort I caught the top of the wall, and scrambling like a cat, I drew myself up. I was now on a sort of causeway, and before me I saw a dim light. Blind and dizzy, I ran on, staggered, and fell, rising, covered with dust and blood.

"Halt!" a voice called out from before me. The words sounded like a voice from heaven. A blaze of light seemed to enwrap me, and I shouted with joy.

"Qui va la?" The rattle of musketry, the flash of steel before my eyes. Instinctively I stopped, though close behind me came a rush of my pursuers.

Another word or two, and out from a gateway poured, as it seemed to me, a tide of red and blue as the guard turned out. All around seemed blazing with light, and the flash of steel, the clink and rattle of arms, and the loud, harsh voices of command. As I fell forward, utterly exhausted, a soldier caught me. I looked behind me in dreadful expectation, and saw the mass of dark forms disappearing into the night. Then I must have fainted.

When I recovered my senses I was in the guard room. They gave me brandy, and after a while I was able to tell them something of what had passed. Then a commissary of police appeared, apparently out of the empty air, as is the way of the Parisian police officer. He listened attentively, and then had a moment's consultation with the officer in command. Apparently they were agreed, for they asked me if I was ready to go with them.

"Where to?" I asked, rising to go.

"Back to the trash piles. We shall, perhaps, catch them yet!"

"I shall try!" I said.

He eyed me for a moment keenly, and said, "Would you like to wait a while or till tomorrow, young Englishman?"

This touched me to the quick, as perhaps he intended, and I jumped to my feet. "I'll come now!" I said. "Right now! An Englishman is always ready for his duty!"

The commissary was a good fellow, as well as a shrewd one; he slapped my shoulder kindly. "Brave garcon!" he said. "Forgive me, but I knew what would do you most good. The guard is ready. Come!"

Passing right through the guard room, and then a long, vaulted passage, we were out into the night. A few of the men in front had powerful lanterns. Through courtyards and down a sloping way we marched out through a low archway to a sunken road, the same one that I'd seen in my flight. The order was given to get at the double, and with a quick, springing stride that was a half-run half-walk, the soldiers went swiftly along.

I felt my strength renewed again—such is the difference between hunter and hunted. A very short distance took us to a low-lying pontoon bridge that went across the stream. Some effort had evidently been made to damage it, for the ropes had all been cut, and one of the chains had been broken.

I heard the officer say to the commissary, "We're just in time! A few more minutes and they would have destroyed the bridge. Forward, quicker still!" We moved onward. Again we reached a pontoon on the winding stream, and as we came up we heard the hollow boom of the metal drums as the efforts to destroy the bridge was again renewed. A word of command was given, and several men raised their rifles.

"Fire!" A volley rang out. There was a muffled cry and the dark forms dispersed. But the damage had been done, and we saw the far end of the pontoon swing into the stream. This was a serious delay, and it was nearly an hour before we hung more ropes and restored the bridge sufficiently to allow us to cross.

We renewed the chase. Quickly we went towards the trash piles. After a time we came to a place that I knew. There were the remains of a fire—a few smoldering wood ashes still cast a red glow—but the bulk of the ashes were cold. I knew the site of the hut and the hill behind it up which I'd rushed, and in the flickering glow the eyes of the rats still shone with a sort of phosphorescence. The commissary spoke a word to the officer, and he cried out, "Halt!" to the men.

The soldiers were ordered to spread out and keep watch, and then we commenced to examine the ruins. The commissary himself began to lift away the charred boards and rubbish, the soldiers then taking them and piling it all together.

Presently, he started back, then beckoned me. "See!" he said.

It was a gruesome sight. There lay a skeleton face down, a woman by the look of it, an old woman by the coarse fiber of the bone. Between the ribs rose a long spike, like a dagger made from a butcher's sharpening knife, its keen point buried in her spine.

"You will observe," the commissary said to the officer and myself as he took out his note book, "that the woman must have fallen on her dagger. The rats are many here. See their eyes glistening among that pile of bones? And you will also notice…" He placed his hand on the skeleton and I shuddered. "That but little time was lost by them, for the bones are scarcely cold!"

There was no other sign of any one near, living or dead, so deploying again into a line, the soldiers and myself moved on. Presently we came to the hut made of the old wardrobe. We approached. In five of the six compartments were old men sleeping so soundly that even the glare of the lanterns didn't wake them. Old and grim and grizzled they looked, with their gaunt, wrinkled, bronzed faces and their white moustaches and a few beards.

The officer called out harshly and loudly a word of command, and in an instant each one of the old men was on his feet before us and standing at attention!

"Why are you here?" the commissary demanded.

"We sleep," was the answer.

"Where are the others?" the commissary asked.

"Gone to work."

"And you?"

"We're on guard!"

"Peste!" laughed the officer grimly, as he looked at the old men one after the other in the face, then added with cool deliberate cruelty, "Asleep on duty! Is this the manner of the Old Guard? No wonder then a Waterloo!"

By the gleam of the lantern I saw the grim old faces grow deadly pale, and almost shuddered at the look in the eyes of the old men as the laugh of the soldiers echoed the grim pleasantry of the officer. In that moment I felt some measure of avengement.

For a moment the old men looked as if they would throw themselves on the swords of the soldiers, but years of their life had schooled them and they remained still.

"You're but five," the commissary said. "Where is the sixth?" The answer came with a grim chuckle.

"He's there!" The speaker pointed to the bottom of the wardrobe. "He died last night. You won't find much of him. The burial of the rats is quick!"

The commissary stooped and looked in. Then he turned to the officer and said calmly, "We may as well go back. No trace here now; nothing to prove that the man was the one wounded by your soldiers' bullets! Probably this lot murdered him to cover up the trace. See!" Again he stooped and placed his hands on the skeleton. "The rats work quickly and there are many. These bones are still warm!"

I shuddered, as did many of the soldiers around me. I thought how if I'd been caught by my pursuers and murdered, my body would have been left to the rats, to quickly be devoured, leaving nothing but bones and a few shreds of cloth. A chilling way to go for any man, whether he be a coward or filled with courage. I looked out at the trash piles, covered in moonlight and saw what to me seemed like a thousand beady eyes. They were all out there, waiting for their next meal, ready to pounce if given the opportunity.

"Form up!" the officer ordered. Within a minute, with the lanterns swinging in front and the manacled veterans in their midst, the soldiers and myself steadily left the trash piles and turned backward to the fortress of Bicetre.

My year of probation has long since ended, and Alice is now my wife. But when I look back upon that trying twelve months, one of the most vivid incidents that I can recalls is the one associated with my visit to the City of Trash.

BENEATH THE CITY

ANTHONY GIANGREGORIO

The moon hung low over New York City one night in May in the year 1970.

Susan Carson was in town for a week with friends and had just left her hotel. She was on the way to a local nightclub to meet her girlfriends, where she planned to celebrate the breakup of her now ex-boyfriend Chad, who had been controlling and far too protective of her. An independent woman, Susan prided herself on not needing anyone to watch over her.

But if she had known what the night would bring, no doubt she would have run back to her hotel, locked her door, and hid under the covers of her bed until morning, where she would then have high-tailed it back home, never to see the big city again.

But the future couldn't be seen as Susan walked down 38th Street, a skip to her step and a smile on her lips, her frilly yellow dress bouncing about her legs.

"Well, well, don't you look happy," a voice called out from Susan's left as she strolled happily down the street. She was a few months past twenty-one and the world was her oyster.

Turning to face the voice, she saw a young man about her age standing in the doorway of a small storefront. He was very handsome, with light brown hair, a hint of a mustache and dark blue eyes.

Feeling happy and playful, Susan decided a little light flirting would be just the thing to pass the time as she strutted by him. "I am happy," she replied with a laugh. "I just broke up with my asshole of a boyfriend and I plan on having a wonderful night at the club with my girlfriends."

"Oh really?" the man said. "I'm free tonight. Maybe I could tag along?" he asked as he stepped out of the alcove and began walking beside Susan. She felt safe on the sidewalk as hundreds of people moved around her, each on their own errands.

"Thank you, handsome, but not tonight. Tonight is for girls only." She stopped walking, pulled a pen from her purse, and took the man's hand, then began writing on his palm. "But give me a call when you're in my neck of the woods and maybe we can get together."

"Thanks, I'll do that," the man said as he looked down at the seven digit phone number scrawled hastily in his palm. He looked up to see her receding back. "Wait, what's your name?" he called out.

"Susan," she replied over her shoulder, her voice playful.

"I'm Michael," he said but then she turned a corner and was gone. But no sooner did she disappear than he decided he couldn't let her get away, so he began jogging after her.

Meanwhile, Susan had began walking up the next street, this one not as well-traveled as 38th. It was as she passed by an open alleyway that she heard something that caught her attention—the sound of a low moan.

"Hello? Is someone down there?" she called into the shadows of the alley. Steam filled the air from an errant pipe and the odor of garbage was strong.

Deep in the shadows in the center of the alley, the darkness shifted and once more a low moan floated on the night air.

"Hello, are you all right? Should I call the police?" Susan was from a small town where everyone helped each other. Naïve in the big city, she couldn't imagine someone wanting to hurt her, despite the warnings she'd received from her parents before leaving on her vacation. This naiveté now was what allowed her to enter the alley, when someone that had lived in the city their entire life would have turned and run away.

It was as she entered the alley and took only a few steps that she detected another odor mixed in with that of garbage. It was dank, musty, animalistic…and very strange, something she couldn't put her finger on.

Peering into the darkness, the steam suffusing the air around her, Susan at first thought she could see a small child, but upon stepping closer, she realized what was before her was the farthest thing possible from a child. The shape was hunched over, only three feet in height, with a bulbous head and small eyes and ears. The nose was nothing but a moist opening that dripped mucous constantly over its slit of a mouth.

Suddenly, more of the small shapes appeared all around her, and before she had a chance to cry out, they were on her, pulling her to the ground, covering her mouth with their small hands. She felt herself being dragged across the ground, heard the sound of the manhole cover that led into the sewer being removed, and then she was pulled into the circular opening. She managed to jerk her head to the side, and as her mouth became free, she let out one quick scream before tiny hands once more covered her mouth, pressing her lips against her teeth so hard that she tasted blood.

The manhole cover was pulled back into the hole, and as she strained to look up at the night sky, she watched the few stars out that evening disappear as the steel cover seated with a dull thud, the sound to her like a gong sealing her fate, whatever it might be.

Michael reached the alleyway Susan had gone down just as the manhole cover stopped moving. Running into the steam and shadows, he was shocked to find the alleyway empty.

"I know she went down here, I saw her go this way," he said as he looked around. His eyes searched each trashcan and the two filthy dumpsters nearby but nothing seemed amiss. He was about to give up when he spotted a small piece of yellow material on the ground. It was caught between the manhole cover, and when he tried to pull it out, the material wouldn't budge. The only way it could have happened was if the cover had been removed.

He quickly searched for something to pry the manhole cover off and found a bent tire iron behind a trashcan. It took only minutes to remove the steel cover and roll it to the side, where it clanged loudly. As he peered into the darkness of the sewer, he reached down for the handgun strapped to his body under his jacket. Once more he was glad he carried a weapon, knowing the streets of New York were far from safe. He debated going for help, to try and find a passing cop, but in the end decided there wasn't time.

As he began climbing down, he hoped he was making the right choice.

The sewer was dry, thanks to the lack of rain recently, and only a few inches of scum-coated water lined the tunnel. Susan opened her eyes to find herself being dragged through the fetid water, her dress quickly becoming soaked with the foul liquid. But that wasn't what caused her to scream in horror behind the gag over her mouth. What caused her to cry out were the small creatures that had bound her hands and were now dragging her somewhere she knew she didn't want to go. Struggling to get free of the ropes around her neck and hands, they only became tighter. One of the creatures glared at her, the warning clear: Stop struggling…or else.

Knowing she had no choice but to obey, she stopped moving, but still gently tested the strength of the creatures as they dragged her through the muck. They weren't strong individually, but there were many of them and their combined strength easily overpowered her.

One of the creatures suddenly tripped and she found herself free for the moment as the ropes fell to the ground. Knowing she had to act, her heart in her throat from fear, she turned and began running in the direction she thought was freedom.

Susan had managed to run no more than five feet before a large rat jumped into her path, its eyes seeming to glow in the darkness. It reared on its hind legs and slashed at Susan, causing her to fall backwards. The hesitation in her escape was enough for the creatures to reach her and they re-secured their grip on her ropes, now also tying her legs so she couldn't run. She was then hoisted onto their shoulders and carried. The rat watched her being taken away, and when it was sure she was gone, it turned and loped away into the darkness.

Susan reached up and pulled her gag from her mouth and let out a scream filled with terror and anguish. It wasn't long before her mouth was covered once more, but the scream echoed through the dark tunnels.

But the creatures knew there was no one to hear her cries but the rats.

Michael's shoes splashed down in the low water and he cursed as the muck coated the sides. The shoes were new and they would be fated for the trash after his little excursion into the sewers.

When Susan had let out a scream she had already been taken far from the where he stood and her scream echoed amongst the tunnels, faint and inaudible.

But though faint, it was the clue Michael needed to know in which direction to set off on her trail. Moving quickly, he began running through the tunnels, careful not to strike his head on low protuberances, only the dim light that filtered in through storm drains and the holes in the numerous manhole covers lighting the way. His shoes quickly began saturated with slimy water and each step was a squishy affair that made him cringe, but ever onward he moved, knowing Susan was in desperate need of rescue.

He quickly became lost, despite his best intentions to remember the twisting, winding tunnels, and though the light grew worse, his eyes became adjusted to the gloom. Rounding a sharp corner, he came face to face with a large sewer rat, one twice the size of a normal housecat.

"Jesus, look at the size of it," he hissed as the rodent slashed the air before it, wanting to lunge at Michael.

But Michael was faster. Still carrying the tire iron, he jumped forward and swiped at the foul rodent with the tool, managing to strike its back and send it toppling into the dark. The rat rolled in the muck and got to its feet instantly, its eyes glowing in the gloom, its teeth flashing as whiskers flicked up and down.

"Get out of here, you bastard, or I'll crack your damn head open," Michael warned as he waved the tire iron before him menacingly.

As if the rat knew it was no match for the human, it swiped the air one last time with its claws and then retreated into the darkness, its long trail the last to be seen before the shadows swallowed it whole. Michael fought down a shiver and moved on, racing after Susan, his mind conjuring up images of the terrible fate she must be suffering.

Who had taken her? What did they want? Michael had yet to see the little creatures that had captured Susan, and so far only had thoughts of more mundane enemies.

He came to a section of the sewers where a hole had been broken in the tunnel wall. Seeing the signs of a disturbance, he entered the hole and found himself in a cavern much older than the sewer system beneath New York. Unbeknownst to Michael, the catacombs went on for miles.

Claws scratching on the rocks behind and on both sides of him caused Michael to turn to look. Before him were more rats, these also good-sized specimens.

"Get back, you evil bastards," he hissed and began swiping at them with the tire iron. One dodged his blow but another was caught right on its back. The sound of its spine cracking filled the catacomb, quickly followed by the screeches of the dying rat.

Like a dinner bell had been rung, the other rats jumped on their fallen brother, tearing and rending its fur and flesh from its bones. Michael used the opportunity to escape them, moving ever deeper underground, hoping he was still going the right way to find Susan.

More rats scuttled around his feet, but they only ran past him, the smell of fresh blood from the killed rat strong in the air. For a time he simply walked, careful not to trip and fall. The walls were strangely luminescent and he found he could see. He tried not to think about what would happen if the light was gone completely. Trapped underground, in the darkness, no doubt he would never find his way back to the surface.

Then he heard sounds, and as he focused on them, he caught the hint of a woman's shriek before it was muffled.

"Susan? It has to be her," he said under his breath. Quickening his pace as hope filled him with a surge of energy, he moved even deeper beneath the city.

While Michael searched desperately through the winding catacombs, Susan was being carried even deeper into the ancient tunnels.

The creatures chattered to each other, and Susan quickly realized it wasn't just noise but was the way they communicated. She also found she could see thanks to the luminescent walls.

Rats were everywhere, following the creatures and their prisoner. A few times Susan had to kick out with her feet to make the rats leave her alone. It was hard thanks to her bindings but the rats were skittish and even a small gesture of movement seemed to be enough to make them leave her alone. Unknown to her, the rats knew Susan wasn't for them, that she was destined for something far more sinister.

Eventually the catacombs opened up to a wide-open cavern and she was unceremoniously dropped in the center. The creatures then left her, each moving off into the shadows. Susan pulled the gag from her mouth and began to scream, but deep down she knew why she was allowed to. Hundreds of feet below the city, who could hear her cries for help?

Despite this, she yelled and screamed until she was hoarse, knowing that was all she had the power to do.

Hopelessly lost, Michael stopped before he entered a tunnel to his right, instead going to one on his left now that he heard Susan's screams.

"It's her. Thank God I heard her or I would have gone off in the wrong direction. I would never have found her otherwise." His voice echoed in the darkness and he felt a chill run down his back. It was so quiet down here, or had been until Susan had cried out. Now he had a definite direction to go and he picked up his pace yet again. The tire iron was held out before him like a sword, ready for any signs of an attack, from either rats or anything else that called the catacombs its home. Images of monsters and devils filled Michael's head and he had to push it down for fear of going mad. The glowing green walls were his only companions…that and the few rats that ventured out of their holes in the walls to investigate the intruder into their home. But each time they would withdraw when Michael swiped at them with the tire iron.

Suddenly, a rat the size of a medium-sized dog appeared in the tunnel and began to move forward. Michael, acting fast, pulled his gun and fired two quick shots, wounding the rat with the first bullet and killing it with the second. The carcass was thrown back against the wall where it began to twitch as blood seeped from the bullet wounds. Michael ran past it on his way towards Susan's screams. As his footsteps receded down the tunnel, smaller rats appeared and soon began to feed on their dead, larger brother.

Susan heard the gunshots and it filled her with hope. Someone was down here, perhaps searching for her. Was it the police? It didn't matter. It was a lifeline out of this nightmare she now found herself in and she began to scream once more, straining her lungs as she called out for help.

The creatures appeared and picked her up, ignoring her shrieks of protests. They began carrying her again, down a dark corridor and into yet another open cavern.

Once more she was dropped heavily to the floor, the creatures moving off and leaving her alone. At first she only could focus on her body, and how her arms hurt her the way they were bound, but as she repositioned herself to be more comfortable, a sixth sense told her she wasn't alone. Slowly, she sat up, and it was as she turned around to face behind her that she saw that indeed she wasn't alone in the large chamber.

For sitting on a throne of stone that had been cut out of the very rock was a monstrosity that shouldn't exist, nay, could not exist in the normal world she lived in.

But how could Susan ignore what was right in front of her, even when the impossible became reality?

She knew then why she had been brought to this chamber before the monster. She was an offering, a tribute, a sacrifice, and her life was forfeit with no chance of escape. Trussed up like a cow ready for the slaughter, she could only stare at the thing with her mouth hanging open, too terrified to even call out for help anymore.

The giant rat shifted on its throne, its nose twitching as it sniffed the air.

It had to be twice Susan's size if not larger, its long tale trailing away from it and into the darkness behind the throne. Its claws were long and sharp and Susan knew it would be a simple task for the large rat to eviscerate her. It was all she could do not to void her bladder right there, though her body trembled in fear.

The rat shifted on its throne and leaned forward, coming down onto its front paws so it was on all fours. Even like this its head would have been even with Susan's head if she had been standing. The large mouth opened wide, incisors dripping saliva in anticipation of the feast to come, and just as it prepared to lunge at the tender morsel before it, Michael burst into the chamber, his gun in his hand.

Letting out a few choice curses, he regained his composure quickly despite seeing the impossible before him. Taking in the scene instantly, he knew Susan's life was hanging by a thread. Running towards her, he began shooting the giant rat, and continued to do so until his gun clicked dry.

The rat absorbed the bullets, squealing loudly as it jumped back and contorted into a ball. One bullet struck its stomach, another its chest, and yet another its neck, wounding it terribly but still not killing it.

"Michael!" Susan cried out, not believing that the man she had flirted with in the street was the person saving her...or trying to.

Holstering his empty gun, Michael ran at the rat, jumped onto its side as it lay on the ground, and used the tire iron like a sword, stabbing the giant rat in its left eye, to then force the weapon deep into its head. The metal slid into the eye socket until it pierced the brain, only stopping when the tip struck the inside of the skull.

The rat spasmed once and went still. Jumping off the carcass, Michael ran to Susan and quickly undid the bonds on her hands, then with her help, they undid the ropes securing her legs.

"Michael I…" she began but he cut her off.

"Later, right now we need to get out of here."

Already dark shapes could be seen on the edges of the cavern. Remembering the creatures that had brought her to this foul place, Susan couldn't have agreed more.

"This way, I think I came in here," Michael said and began leading Susan out of the catacombs.

The trek to the surface was long and arduous but in time they found the entry into the sewer system and from there it was easy to reach the streets above.

As they walked down the street hand in hand, Susan suddenly broke away from him and hopped on a passing bus just as it was pulling away from the curb.

"Wait," Michael called out. "I saved you, don't I get a reward?" he called after her as she stood in the bus' doorway, the bus driver annoyed she was there, as he wanted to close the door.

"Of course you will. I gave you my number already," she laughed. "Call me in a few days and I'll give you such a reward you'll never forget it." There was a twinkle in her eye of the pleasures to come. She felt so alive. The past few hours were like a terrible dream, and the horror was slowly fading away. Perhaps when she slept in future days, nightmares would come, but for the moment she was happy.

Michael watched her go, his thoughts already on the reward she promised. But as he looked down at his palm where Susan had written her number, he saw that only one number remained, the rest having worn off from his exertions in the sewer and catacombs.

Looking up, he prepared to run after the bus, to catch Susan before it was too late, but the bus was already down the street and too far away to reach.

She was gone and there was no way to ever find her again. He didn't even know her last name.

At first he felt angry, but then as he watched the bus turn the corner and disappear from sight, he began to smile.

"Ah well, there's always next time," he said with a chuckle, and turning, began to walk away.

ROTTEN FOOD

MARIAH DEITRICK

"Being a slave to the night doesn't mean I have to be a monster," I said, setting my food free.

"But it's only a rat, Cole," Sean said.

I shrugged. "It's still a living creature."

Sean pointed at the wobbly rat. "Leaving it half-dead is better?"

"He'll be fine in a few hours," I assured him. "I never take enough blood to kill them."

Shaking his head, he said, "You realize you'd be doing humans a favor by killing the rodents, right?"

I sighed. I was sick of repeating myself night after night. That was why I always hunted alone. But Sean was a good kid, so I didn't hesitate to bring him along when he'd asked if I could teach him how to stop feeding on humans. He was the newest member of our coven and one of the few I could tolerate. But even he couldn't understand why I went against my nature and didn't kill any living creature. No one could. I'm a vampire. Vampires are supposed to be wicked creatures of the night, sucking the life out of innocent humans. I wasn't that way, so who was I to judge rats just because humans found them repulsive? I'm sure humans would feel the same about me if they knew I existed.

"Do you want to learn or not?" I asked, secretly hoping he changed his mind so I could feed and go home. The sun would rise soon and the city was waking, not that New York really ever slept, but I could handle a few humans at a time. What I couldn't deal with was the thousands of humans that would soon fill the sidewalks, roads, and shops.

I've spent centuries depriving myself of human blood merely by avoiding the entire race as much as possible. If I encountered a herd of them while starving, it would be disastrous. I could wipe out thousands before anyone had a clue what was happening.

Sean put his hands up. "Okay, okay. I'll behave."

"Since I've wasted all night answering your stupid questions," I said, "we'll have to go into the sewer to feed." I pointed at the manhole cover a few feet away from us.

"Really, Cole? You go in the sewer?" Sean wrinkled his nose.

I understood his disgust. I detested the sewer myself. I mean, wasn't it bad enough I resorted to sucking on a rat's neck to survive? Did I really need to have my food covered in human waste, too?

Times like this made me consider leaving the coven. At least if I was alone, I could stay in a place longer than a week. Besides, I preferred smaller towns. For one, they had a buffet of animals for me to feast on. Plus, I could fill up on a cow or deer in a matter of minutes and have the rest of the night free to find the company of a woman, which I hadn't done in…well…too long to count. But none of that mattered at the moment. Right then, we only needed to focus on feeding, beating the sun, and avoiding humans.

"Yep. We're really going in there." I yanked up the cover. "Now's your chance to back out."

He folded his arms across his chest. "Give me a little credit. I'm damn near invincible. I think I can handle dropping down a hole and hunting rats."

I chuckled and gestured for him to go first. "Be my guest."

Ignoring the ladder, Sean leapt down the hole and landed with a splash. "Oh man, this is horrible," he called up.

Normally, I would have climbed down the ladder, but Sean wasn't going to outdo me in my own territory, so I gracefully stepped off the edge, staying as close to the wall as possible so I wouldn't land in the disgusting water below.

Sean waded through the muck to join me on the small ledge. "How do you find the rodents down here? All I smell is shit."

"You need to rely on your other senses."

"Hunting humans is so much easier," he complained, wringing out his shirt.

"Don't start," I warned. "We don't have time to discuss this again."

He shrugged. "I'm just saying."

"Focus," I snapped. "We need to be quiet and listen."

Sean closed his eyes and plugged his nose. Clearly relying on only his ears was difficult for him. The urge to protect ourselves at all cost was a tough instinct to turn off, but we weren't in danger now. As long as we used our ears, we would avoid any of the homeless lurking around.

Once Sean finally closed his mouth, I had no problem detecting my prey. They scratched and squeaked not far from where we stood. From the sound of the commotion, I'd say there was a nest of a hundred or so. That number could easily satisfy us both for the day.

My mouth watered and my throat burned. Forgetting about training Sean, I darted toward the creatures that offered to quench my thirst.

"Wait up!" Sean called, having no problem keeping up with me as I raced through the sewers.

As the sound of our prey grew more pronounced, I watched Sean war with his instincts and his disgust for the rats. His body crouched automatically, ready to pounce, but he wrinkled his nose and shook his head. I might have laughed at him if my throat wasn't on fire and any amount of breathing fueled the blaze.

I waved him forward. The nest wasn't far. I could smell the blood above the stench of the sewer. The scent wasn't as alluring as human blood, but Sean's body would react if he wasn't distracted by me.

Quietly, Sean slipped into the darkened tunnel. I had to battle my own hunger so I wouldn't follow him right away. The first hunt was the most important. He needed a few minutes to feed alone, without distractions, or he could completely freak out and scare the rats. I, for one, didn't want to go home hungry when I was this close to food.

I listened closely to the sounds around me, waiting for my cue. The minute I smelled fresh blood and heard the squeal of rats as they scurried away, I planned on making my entrance.

After waiting for ten agonizing minutes, Sean screeched, "Cole, help me!" His plea made my hair stand on end. If he was in trouble and needed my help, that meant he was up against something that could actually harm him. The only thing I knew that could be that dangerous to us was a werewolf, but the moon was only half full, and I hadn't seen one in centuries.

Slowly, I moved toward the danger, sniffing the air for the scent of the threat. Sean's scent was the first one I recognized because his trail was the freshest. Then came the sewer and the rats, but nothing else. I could detect nothing out of the ordinary, nothing to put my senses on alert.

"Sean!" I called. No answer.

If this was his idea of a joke, it wasn't funny. We didn't have time for games. I walked back and forth over and over, trying to pick up a good scent trail. It was odd. I couldn't figure out exactly where he went. His scent stopped halfway down the tunnel. I found nothing to lead me to believe he wasn't in that area hiding somewhere, which irritated me.

"Come on, Sean. This isn't funny." My words came out as a growl; this was absurd. I never should have allowed him to come along after all the questions he'd asked earlier. He made it clear that he didn't want to participate in my lifestyle. Why didn't I send him on his way when I had the chance? Forget it. I didn't need to hunt him down. He knew his way back to the coven.

I took a couple of deep breaths to calm myself—I didn't need the air—and listened to the sounds around me. The air held a strange flavor that distracted me. The taste of copper made my body stiffen. When I sniffed, a horrible rotting flesh smell burned my nostrils. My mouth dried, the flame in my throat vanished, and I dropped into a hunting crouch automatically. I could sense no danger, but I knew exactly what the potent smell was— vampire blood. Humans would never pick up the stench, but I could.

"Sean!" I called again. "This better not be a joke, or I'll kill you myself. Sean!"

Someone groaned. "Down here."

I glanced into the dark, murky water to find Sean's head barely breaking the surface. "What the hell are you doing down there?" I asked, letting my irritation and annoyance saturate every word.

"They got me," he said, his voice no more than a whisper. If it weren't for my impeccable hearing, I might not have been able to make out the words at all.

"What?" I asked, glancing around me, suddenly on guard.

"The rats," he said. "The rats attacked me."

I narrowed my eyes at him as anger flared up inside me. "I don't know what kind of fucked-up game you think you're playing, but it's not funny. You can find your own way out of here." I knew that wasn't actually a threat. Sean could find his way out just as easily as I could, but he was lucky I didn't hop down and rip him apart. If I didn't go now, I might not be able to stop myself.

I turned to leave him when he shouted, "Wait! I'm telling the truth. I can prove it to you if you get me out of this disgusting water."

With a sigh, I folded my arms across my chest. I didn't see any rats around. If they attacked him, where did they go?

"You expect me to believe that a few little rodents ganged up on you and tossed you in the water?" I raised an eyebrow skeptically.

He shook his head. "I jumped down here myself to get away from them, but not before they ate my fucking feet off. Shit. I can't heal from that, can I?" His voice rose with panic. "I mean, my feet won't grow back. How can I go the rest of my existence without feet? I'll never be able to hunt again."

I knew at that moment that Sean was telling the truth. Maybe not about the rats attacking him, but something had. Even Sean wouldn't take a prank that far, but I still wasn't convinced rats had damaged him. I'd have to look at the wounds to determine the cause.

Without a word, I leapt down next to him and grabbed his leg out of the water to inspect his foot. The rotten flesh smell almost knocked me over the minute his gnawed ankles left the water. He was right. His feet were completely gone. Bone protruded out of where his foot once was, and what looked like ground-up meat dangled around it. Whatever caused the damage had small sharp teeth. I had to concentrate not to cringe.

"It's bad, huh?" Sean asked.

"Rats did this?" I avoided his question, hoping to prevent him from completely freaking out before I had all the details.

"Yes," he said. "They came from nowhere. I could hear and smell them, but I didn't see them until they were on top of me."

"Odd," I mused. Rats weren't fast or invisible. With Sean's sharpened eyesight, he should have spotted them way before they were close enough to take a chunk out of him.

"I know," Sean agreed.

Nails scraped against metal pipes overhead. I glanced up at the exact moment a rat lost its grip on the slippery pipe and dropped on my face. Its nails dug into my cheeks. As I grabbed it and tossed it to the ground, another fell onto the back of my neck, then another dropped on my shoulder. They kept coming. I'd grab one and chuck it away only to have another land on me, sinking its teeth and claws into my skin over and over again. Blood oozed from the wounds the rats inflicted on my face and neck.

I hurled more to the ground as I snatched Sean out of the water, tossed him over my shoulder, and raced away from the bombarding rain of rats.

"Leave me!" Sean said.

"No."

"Cole, I can't live like this. Leave me behind and go."

Because there was no way I could ever leave him behind, I ignored him and kept running. After all, my lifestyle was what had landed him here in the first place. Sure, he wanted to come along, but that didn't matter. I should have sent him away like my gut told me to do all night.

When I no longer heard the sound of splashing rats behind us, I jumped out of the water. "Not much farther," I said.

Sean groaned in answer as his mangled leg stumps flapped against me. I knew he had to be in pain, not from the wounds, but the loss of blood. His throat had to be on fire, and his skin probably burned as the blood left his veins.

I starved myself once. The pain was more than I could bear, and I knew it wouldn't stop until I fed. Sean needed to eat or he'd only get worse.

When I stumbled across a lonely rat in my path, I sat Sean down and scooped it up. "Hurry!" I said, shoving the rat at him. "You need this."

Sean took it with shaky hands and bit down on the small neck. Almost the instant his teeth broke through flesh, he yanked his head away and spit the blood out.

"I told you it wouldn't taste the same as human blood," I said, "but it's not that bad."

"Yes, it is." He continued to spit, then wiped his mouth with the back of his hand.

Since the wound was still oozing blood, I ran my index finger across it and tasted for myself. Ugh! Sean was right. I spit and tossed the rat into the water below. "It's like sucking on a zombie's neck," I said, giving Sean the best description I could come up with for the foul flavor of the rat's blood.

"Pretty accurate," Sean agreed. "So, that's not normal?"

I shook my head. "No."

A few feet away another rat was coming toward us. In a flash, I picked it up, bit into its neck, and instantly regretted it. It tasted just as bad as the other one. I flipped the squirming rat back and forth in my hands, examining the creature. I found nothing out of place with it.

Instead of chucking it into the water like the last one, I set this one on the ledge in front of me and watched. Its whiskers twitched as it sniffed the air.

"What are you doing?" Sean asked. "Shouldn't we be going?" For someone who wanted to be left behind only moments ago, he sure was in a hurry to leave now. But I needed to figure this out. I'd been hunting the rats every night for months. How could they possibly have changed that quickly, and overnight? But Sean was right. With his injuries, we didn't have time to waste playing with the vermin. He needed to feed and it was going to take more than a couple of rats to help him.

With a sigh, I kicked the rodent off the ledge and pushed back my disgust for feeding on humans. I had no choice but to hunt one down for Sean.

"I'll find you food once we're out of here," I said as I lifted him from the ground.

"No," Sean objected. "Take me back to the coven. I'll feed later."

I rolled my eyes. "Spoken like a true newborn," I said. "You have no idea what it's like to starve." But I did. I wouldn't let him endure the agony I'd once put myself through.

As a vampire, your body fought to quench its thirst. Your veins rubbed like sandpaper under your skin, your motionless heart squeezed in your chest, and every single nerve in your body felt as though someone had taken them out and dipped them in acid before putting them back. By midday, Sean would be screaming and writhing in pain. No one would be able to help him until night fell. So no, he couldn't wait.

"Someone else can hunt a human for me," he said.

"There's no time," I said. We'd reached the manhole cover by then. No, there was no time. Sunlight streamed in, glinting off the first three rungs of the ladder. We had to find a different route home, a shadier one, or we were both ash.

I turned back toward the sewer tunnels. If we hurried, and didn't encounter any problems, we might be able to make it to the manhole right outside the apartment building our coven had invaded months ago. No humans lived there anymore, but I might be able to lure one that hung around nearby into the shadows of the alley. But we had to race to make it before the sun climbed any higher in the sky and erased the darkness we desperately needed.

"Where are you going?" Sean asked. I'd forgotten he faced the ground and had no idea how late it actually was.

"The sun is up," I said, cursing myself for allowing our hunt to take so long. I never should have strayed so far from home so late into the night.

Sean squirmed. "We can't go back," he said. "Can't we wait out the day here?"

"Now why hadn't I thought of that?" I said sarcastically. "Maybe because you were chewed on by rats," I growled. My hunger was getting the best of me. I had to get control of it. None of this was Sean's fault. Okay, maybe if he hadn't asked so many damn questions and just fed like I wanted him to, we wouldn't have had to resort to climbing into the sewers. Still, I was as much to blame as he was. After all, I was the mentor in this situation. He only wanted to learn, and I had no right snapping at him like that.

"Sorry," I said.

"No problem, Cole. You're hungry. I get it."

Even though he was in pain and knew he'd never be the same again, Sean still kept his head. I had to give him credit for that. Not many vampires could control their hunger like he was. I should know, I was proof.

"Shouldn't take too long to get out of here," I said as I weaved in and out of tunnels at top speed. I kicked all the rodents we passed without taking the time to inspect them, though I desperately wanted to.

"Humans," Sean whispered, his voice too low for the nearing people to hear.

I sniffed the air, slowing slightly. Homeless humans hung around in the sewer, everyone knew that. However, they always stayed in groups. No way could we slip in and feed on them without someone noticing, especially with Sean in his condition. The humans would flip out, and with the sun out, they had the advantage. We couldn't disappear the way we could at night. Sure, we were much faster, but we were limited in our escape routes.

My throat burned as the scent grew stronger. "We'll take a different way," I said, turning back. I'd avoided humans for so long that I didn't think twice about running away from them.

Sean did. "We should feed down here," he said, his voice harsh. His throat had to feel like he'd consumed a gallon of acid by now. The smell of his rotten blood oozing from his body was faint, which meant he didn't have much blood left to lose.

"There's no time," I said. "We're barely going to make it out as it is. I'll get you a human once we're safely out of here."

Sean growled and wiggled in my arms. His hunger intensified by the scent of human blood in the air. "Now," he demanded. "Or leave me here."

"Damn it, Sean," I snarled and set him down. "Stay here." The only way this could work is if I could lure a human over to me. I only hoped I didn't run into too many at once. No matter how dire the situation, I wasn't ready to take on a horde of humans, not with being so hungry. I didn't have the restraint necessary to stop myself from slaughtering them all.

"Where are you going?" Sean asked.

"Just stay there," I said and followed the scent of the humans at top speed. I didn't slow until I heard their voices. I tried to determine how many of them I'd stumbled upon and how to go about getting their attention when I recognized another sound. Scratching and squeaking, mingled with the humans' conversations.

Although the people didn't seem frantic or in danger, I rushed into the small section of sewer the humans were using as a home. Two men, a woman and a child sat on beds made from cardboard and newspaper. I was instantly struck with a pang of guilt for what I was about to do.

Although I knew I should leave and find others for Sean, it was too late. The woman gasped and the man with a long, snarled beard and hair to his shoulders said, "This spot's taken, pal."

I put my hands up as if in surrender. "I'm sorry," I said, and I was. "My friend is hurt. Something attacked him." That's when I remembered the sound of rats mixed with their voices. I glanced around. My head cocked to the side when I realized the rodents had stopped whatever they were doing before I'd barged in and were now staring back at me. Their noses twitched as they sniffed the air.

"We can't help you," the bearded man said. "You need to leave."

I nodded, but I wasn't really paying attention to him or the other humans. The rats had shifted slightly, stalking toward me. They weren't scurrying away as most did. These appeared to be hunting me. Each step they took toward me was like a cat approaching its prey. Any second they would pounce on me. I took a step back, still curious about the vermin. What was making them target me and not the humans? Didn't they know the people in the room were the easiest prey? Of course they didn't, they were rats for crying out loud.

I shook my head. "Sorry," I said again. "I really could use your help. I just need to get him out of here and to a hospital. If..."

"I'll help you out, but you're on your own after that," the bearded man interrupted.

"Harold!" the woman scolded. "You can't."

While the two discussed the issues with him leaving the others alone, I kept my eyes on the rats. Experimentally, I took a step to the left. Ever so slightly, each rodent shifted just enough to keep me in their path.

"Momma," the little girl said, tugging at her mother's tattered shirt and pointing at the rats. Her mother ignored her, but the little girl continued to watch the rodents as I moved this way and that. They always followed me, never taking their beady little eyes off me. Even the arguing going on around them didn't slow their advance.

"Listen…I really need to get going," I said, but I fully intended on taking a rat with me. I didn't want to have anyone watch an attack, but I had to examine one of them better.

"Yes," the man said. "The sooner you're out of here, the more comfortable my family will be."

The woman gave the man a disapproving look. "Please, Harold, don't go," she whispered.

"Jake, you're in charge while I'm gone," Harold told the other man, who was actually no more than a boy. He couldn't have been more than eighteen, but he was tall and muscular. Hell, he was bigger than I was, not that his size mattered. He was still no match for me.

"Yes, sir," Jake said.

I wondered why only the little girl had noticed the rats' behavior toward me. Maybe they were just so used to living with them that they didn't bother paying attention to the vermin anymore. Even when the rats sped up and started to surround me, the only one who looked alarmed was the little girl.

"Momma!" the girl tugged harder on the woman's shirt.

"What, Jess?" the woman snapped, clearly annoyed that her daughter was bothering her.

The little girl jabbed one small finger at the ever-growing group of rats. Though I'd been watching them myself, I hadn't realized how many more had crawled out of the shadows. When I'd entered the area, only a dozen rats were roaming around. Now, there had to be more than double that number. I didn't know where or when they'd snuck in, but I was in trouble if I didn't get away soon.

"We need to go," I said.

Harold and his family stared at the rats with gaping mouths. When one of the rats lunged at me, the woman and girl screamed.

"What the hell is going on?" Harold asked.

I kicked the rat off me only to have another attack from behind. I had to get away. Keeping up a human facade wasn't really feasible at the moment. I had to escape and I didn't have time to slow my pace. To the humans, it probably appeared as though I'd vanished into thin air. I didn't care. I had to get back to Sean and escape the sewer.

The rats' claws scraped stone and metal as they dug in to keep up with me. Though I couldn't see them, I knew they weren't far behind. Thankfully, there were plenty of other ways out of the sewer. Sure, the sun was going to be an issue, but as long as I stuck to the shadows, Sean and I could wait out the day in the basement of an apartment building.

More rats scratched and squeaked throughout the tunnels. They were all around me, but I still couldn't see them.

"Sean!" I'd left him helpless. He'd never be able to fight off an attack in his state.

I pushed myself harder, ignoring the sound of pursuit, which wasn't easy as it grew louder and louder by the second. It sounded as though every rat in New York City had joined forces to hunt me down. The problem was that I still had no explanation for their behavior. I had to get my hands on another one if I was ever going to have an answer, but now was not the time.

"Hurry, Cole!" Sean shouted.

I wasn't far from him. I could smell the blood mingled with his scent, but I also detected the thick aroma of rodent in the air. My body crouched automatically as I ran. The rats were everywhere.

When I finally reached Sean, he was fighting off a handful of rats as they attacked and took chunks out of his flesh every chance they could. I grabbed them, snapped their necks, and tossed them away until Sean was free from their assault.

"Where the hell were you?" he asked.

"Sorry," I said. I never should have left him alone in his condition.

"Where's the human?"

"It didn't work out." I grabbed him and put him over my shoulder.

"What do you mean it didn't work out?" he asked while I ran in the opposite direction of the humans.

"Too many rats," I said. "I had to get the hell out of there."

Sean sighed. "What the hell is going on around here?" he muttered.

"I don't know, but we need to get out of here fast," I said as though it wasn't obvious.

The first exit I came to, I readjusted Sean so he held onto my neck and dangled from my back, thus freeing my hands to climb the ladder easily. We made it to the top in seconds. I shoved the manhole cover out of the way. Sunlight flooded in, burning us both.

Sean cried out as his skin smoldered.

My hands slipped as I flinched away from the light. I recovered quickly, but made a huge mistake. In my effort to stop us from falling, I wasn't careful where I'd grabbed. My fingers melted instantly to the metal rung they gripped as the sunlight heated it. Chunks of flesh stuck to the rung as I pulled free and dropped the six feet to the ground. The impact was so sudden that Sean lost his grip on me and hit the ground with a thud.

"Shit," he groaned.

"Sorry about that." I stared at my gnarled fingers. They'd heal, but it would take a while, and at the moment I didn't have enough blood in my system to heal properly. By the time my fingers were back to normal, the sun would have already claimed all the shadows. "We'll have to wait out the day."

"We can't stay down here," Sean said.

A twinge of guilt struck me as I heard the panic in his voice. "If we go out there…" I pointed at the opening above. "We'll burn to death."

"Well, if we stay down here, those things will gnaw us to death," Sean countered.

I nodded. "I guess we'll have to stay one step ahead of them until nightfall." I knew that wasn't going to be easy. I knew that in a few short hours, Sean would be screaming in agony from his wounds and from not feeding. His cries would echo through the tunnels, leading the horde of rats directly to us. But I couldn't come up with a better option.

Sean sighed. "Just how do you suppose we do that? Look at your hands and my legs," he said.

Squeaks and the scratching of nails grew louder as the rodents came closer. "I guess it's a good thing your hands work and my legs work," I said. "Grab on." I bent down so he could wrap his arms around my neck again. We didn't have time to stick around and argue the best odds of survival. Running was the only option at the moment.

He wrapped his arms around my neck and I took off, winding this way and that through the tunnels, hoping to ditch the rats. No such luck. Every new turn I made brought a new group of rats on our trail.

"This isn't working," Sean said as though I hadn't already known that. I ignored him and continued twisting my way deeper into the sewer, reminding myself we only had to last the day.

As we continued on, the exits became farther and fewer between—not a good sign. It would be ironic that we lasted out the day but ended up with no way out of the sewer. I had to backtrack. I took a sharp left followed by another. I couldn't take the same paths, of course, and I had no problem steering clear of the tunnels with our scent already hanging in the air.

Sean groaned and lost his grip, slipping to the ground. I spun around as he curled up.

"I can't go anymore," he moaned. "The pain is too much."

"You have to," I said. "I'll carry you." I reached down, but the minute my hands touched his skin, he cried out in pain.

"No!" he gasped. "Leave me."

I shook my head. I couldn't just leave him for the rats to devour. I wouldn't. "Remember, this won't last much longer." But I knew his pain was coming much quicker than I thought it would, which meant he'd suffered far worse than I had when I didn't eat.

His face screwed up in pain. "It's too much, Cole. I can't."

"Don't say that. Once you feed, you'll be fine."

Sean shook his head. "No, I won't. I still won't have my feet. I'll never be able to hunt on my own again."

My eyes pricked, but thankfully, vampires weren't capable of crying. He was giving up but I wouldn't let him. "I'll hunt for you. I'll do whatever I have to for you to survive."

"Please, Cole, let me die," he begged. Then his expression changed. I could see hope in his eyes. "You have to kill me."

I stood frozen for a moment while my brain caught up with the words that came out of his mouth. I couldn't even kill an animal, how could I possibly kill him? Ignoring him, I bent down to grab him again.

This time, he grabbed the collar of my shirt. "Please," he whispered.

Before I had a chance to tell him the million reasons why I wouldn't leave him or kill him, the walls around us began to vibrate as dirt rained down from cracks above us.

Sean shoved me back. "Get out of here now! I'll stall them!"

My gaze darted from the walls to the ceiling and back to Sean. A low growl rumbled through my chest in warning to the rats surrounding us. I grabbed Sean, not caring if it hurt him or not. He struck at me over and over, but he was so weak that I hardly felt his assault. Each punch felt more like a leaf dropping from a tree and landing on my shoulder than a fist connecting with my chest.

A horrible scratching that seemed to come from everywhere drowned out Sean's complaints. The sound hurt my ears. It was like a hundred people running their nails down a chalkboard at the same time.

That's when I saw the horde of rats ahead of me. There were so many of them that it appeared the ground was moving. In the desperate haste to get to us, they climbed over each other and fought amongst themselves.

I whirled around, heading away from the horde. Although their legs were much shorter than mine, they kept up easily.

"Cole, look," Sean said, jabbing a weak finger at a small group of six or seven rats ahead.

I crouched down, ready to leap over them, but they turned. They appeared to be going away from the danger as any normal rat would do, and they weren't as quick as the ones behind us. Sean and I overtook them in a matter of seconds. Not one of the rodents even attempted to take a bite out of us. In fact, they cowered away.

We'd just made it past them when high-pitched squeals echoed through the tunnels. I glanced back over my shoulder in time to watch the horde of rats overtake the smaller group. Everything happened so quickly, I almost missed it. The large group of rats didn't kill the others.

They simply sank their teeth in for a brief second, causing their victims to stumble and fall. I thought they were killing each other until the smaller group, one by one, leapt to their feet and joined the attacking mob in pursuit of me. That's when something I hadn't even considered before dawned on me.

"My venom," I muttered. "My venom changed them."

"Impossible," Sean said.

I shook my head and rounded another corner. "They're changing each other, too." Though I couldn't even wrap my head around my own thoughts, it was the only explanation I could come up with.

"No way," Sean said.

Continuing on my path away from the killer rodents, I explained. Good thing I could run for hours without feeling even the slightest bit breathless or talking would have been impossible. "Think about it, Sean. They didn't attack the humans, only us and each other. They're changing each other, and their teeth can penetrate our skin. Other than vampires and werewolves, what other creature can do that?"

Sean's face screwed up in pain and his breath came out in a huff before he spoke through gritted teeth. "Are you suggesting your venom turned them into some kind of vampire-hunting rat mob?"

Okay, when he put it that way, I understood how ridiculous my theory sounded. "Yes," I said, because ridiculous or not, I was positive that was what had happened.

The more I ran, the more rats gathered behind Sean and me. They seemed to pop out of nowhere and continued to claim the *normal* ones as they passed them to join their group.

Since I hadn't managed to turn around when I intended to, the exits had all but vanished. I stumbled on one every now and then, but not nearly as often as I would have liked, and the rats didn't ease up long enough for me to check them anyway. All I could do was keep moving forward.

To make matters worse, Sean started to writhe in my arms and he kept up a nonstop scream of sheer agony.

I knew he wanted me to put him down, but couldn't express the words. I tried to console him, telling him everything would be better soon. Nothing helped, and hope was fading fast.

When I made another sharp right, I ended up in a dead end, with nowhere to go but up. I hadn't expected the tunnels to actually end anywhere, so by the time I recovered from my shock, the entrance was already blocked by hundreds of rats.

"Shit!" I muttered.

Sean's screams broke. "Put…me…down," he gasped. "Run."

I glanced around frantically in search of a solution, but found nothing. The rats lunged, tearing chunks of flesh off my shins and thighs.

I stumbled back but their attack continued. Their razor-sharp teeth sliced easily through my skin, their claws digging in as they tried to climb up my legs. They were so quick it was like being stabbed with a million needles at the same time. I could barely keep hold of Sean, who was screaming again. Eventually I dropped him. I couldn't help it. My instincts to protect myself overrode my need to keep Sean alive.

The rats covered his entire body in seconds. Sean's agonized shrieks ended with a grotesque gurgle that sent a chill through me. I wanted to help him, but he was already gone.

While the rats were distracted, I tried to make my way past them. They engulfed me in seconds, stopping me in my tracks. The screams I heard now came from my own throat as thousands of teeth sliced and tore into my flesh.

I stumbled backwards, tripping over a group behind me and falling to the ground. All I could see was black fur and blood.

They tore fingers from my hands, an eyelid from one of my eyes, and the tip of my nose clean off my face before I had a chance to fight back. I snapped necks, tossed and kicked any in reaching distance until I was back on my feet. Sun or no sun, I had to make a run for it.

I only prayed that when I reached the surface, that shade would be nearby for me to hide in before the sun set me on fire and turned me to ash.

I scrambled up a ladder toward a manhole cover with one hand. Rats clung to me, biting as I went. With my head I shoved the manhole cover off. The sun burned my eyes, face, anywhere it touched.

Despite the pain, I pulled myself out onto the busy street. Cabs honked as I blindly crawled toward shelter. The rats didn't seem to be bothered by the sun at all and more crept out of the sewer.

Women screamed while men yelled, "Call an ambulance!" and "We have to help him," but nobody stepped in to get the rats off me.

I knew the instant my body burst into flames. The pain was so excruciating that it paralyzed me. People shouted around me, and the rats high-tailed it out of there.

Completely immobilized, I watched as the road turned to a black river of rodents. Even through the pain, I knew they were on the hunt for the rest of my coven, but I could do nothing to stop them.

Turning to dust wasn't as quick as movies portray. There was no poof and ash raining down where the vampire had been. Instead, it happened slowly. I watched through watery eyes as my remaining fingers, hands, wrists, and forearms dried out and blew away in the breeze.

Although my body was nearly gone, my mind stayed sharp so I knew exactly what was happening. I understood that the rats I'd fed on for the past few months were getting their revenge on me.

When I could no longer suck in air, I knew my body was gone. For a brief moment, all I could think about was what the poor, unsuspecting onlookers thought about the scene unfolding before them.

Then I realized it didn't matter. I was dying. I'd lived a very long time, not fearing anything, only to be killed by my own food.

With one last burst of heat and pressure that felt like my head was about to explode, everything went black.

MAUSOLIS

ANTHONY ALEXANDER VALADE

That jagged piece of glass; if there was only a way to crawl over to it. This pain is unbearable but if I must lay here until my death, I'll wear it with pride. My brothers, sisters, and lovers must stay strong. A culmination of a life is only a misconception waiting to happen; this world will forever remain even though it's something I'll never obtain again.

Maybe it was the dog, the fall, or maybe it was the way each shotgun shell collided with the walls, creating a portrait of myth disease in rat blood, but maybe minority revolution should be taken into more consideration before being attempted.

Every bone in this freshly opened porous body could possibly be wedging its way out. At this angle I'm watching as red liquid slowly flows away from my body; the tiny river is inching towards the broken glass from one of the above windows. How I wish for even an inch of a sharp object...

I thought the idea could be easy at first: gather some friends and family, hold some meetings and spread the word around. Not a lot of people were interested at that time, but I was handed a little luck when two of our youngest residents wanted to make a new friend. There was no choice other than to take advantage of them, so I created a couple of simple tests for them to accomplish to become my 'friend.' It was hard to tell their smell apart but it was eventually easier when I started to compare their faces instead— one of them had a distinguishing white dot on his forehead.

The first task was to go around spreading word about extermination by the humans. This plan didn't work very well as rats have no comprehension skills when it comes to speaking any language of the humans. Most rats who were told just shrugged it off. We don't believe in a higher power; if extermination was to happen only the king would know and he would handle the situation. Each response made me question my expectations of what I was trying to do. I wanted to 'be' the king.

The aspect was unheard of. Only the chosen would become the next king—the biggest, and most vicious. It almost didn't even matter if he was respected; one floodgate of urination later from him would prove his dominance and then everyone would back down. That's why I never take my place at meetings near the front row; you don't know bad taste till you have to bathe yourself with only your own tongue.

The second plan was one I had to take part in unfortunately. My two light brown friends and I were to break into the local market, a feat that had never been performed by anyone in our lair. When it came time to plan for the deed to be done, I decided a visit to the surface was in order to clear my head.

I remember it was chilly that night with an odd vibrating sound in the air. There were three black objects circling up above, and I made sure to take cover near the base of a lonely tree that was very close to the hole. The lights from the small town in the distance attracted my attention; sometimes in the late afternoon you could get caught up in a couple of waves of the most delicious smells.

Regardless of what the smells were from, they'd make me drool for hours. It was always something I wanted to know more about, so I figured I might as well get two productive things done at once. As I stared into the lights, a chilling feeling came over me, and paranoia began to set in as I slowly scanned the area. Black shadows were still floating up in the sky, but as I turned my attention to the tree, I found a large pair of eyes staring at me.

The moonlight was immediately hidden, leaving me in the dark. In the tree branches was some sort of living creature; its very large oval shape was accompanied by two tiny legs and two giant, flat arms. I watched as the small eyes in the silhouette reflected moonlight inside themselves, making them a pure white in my colorblind eyes. My body began to shake with terror. There was no way I could defend myself from this creature. As I pulled my tail underneath my body and clenched my eyes shut, the creature fell down from the tree with its arms spread wide.

If I didn't know any better, I'd say I was lucky, but unfortunately *I was lucky.* The next thing I felt was a gush of air glide over me and tiny screams from another rat were floating up and away from my ears. As I took myself out of hiding, I stood and watched as the creature climbed straight into the air. Suddenly I was covered in a warm liquid and I could smell her pheromones in it. Her blood rained down onto the ground all around me, followed by her soulless head which had been bitten off at the neck. I'd mated with her several times in the past month. I wasn't the only one, but I thought I felt a special connection between us. Why else would she have followed me out here?

In remembrance I grabbed what was left of her and retreated underground. I buried her head underneath my bed. Her blood dried onto my fur throughout the night, but I had no intention of cleaning it off anytime soon. The surface wasn't safe.

The next day no one asked questions; like it didn't matter. My friends didn't even come for me, in fact, I walked by them several times and they didn't even look at me. I tried waiting all day to see if they would say something, but it felt fruitless so I walked up and attempted to start a conversation, assuming they would recognize my voice.

Apparently it was the nicest greeting they've ever been given because they immediately began humping themselves all over my body. My claw made a pretty nice slice into one of them and they immediately stopped. They told me they thought I was a girl, so angrily I told them how gender challenged they must be while asking what kind of nasty sewer rats they were mating with. An immediate apology from them followed after my last 'I clearly have a penis,' remark.

After letting them know exactly what happened the night before, they were still confused as to why it wasn't safe to cross on the land. Amidst ignoring their inferior questions, I revealed my plan to tunnel our way into town, they didn't seem too impressed at the amount of work, but after I told them what peanut butter was, they were pretty excited.

We began digging three tunnels from our habitat that connected in a circle, this was to divert other rats from finding our tunnel, which was made parallel to the center but only had exits leading to the other tunnels unless you looked at it the right way. The digging continued for several hours until we couldn't go on any longer. To make sure our tunnel wouldn't be compromised, we closed off the entrance with some of the excess dirt. As we returned back to the rest of the habitat, we were stopped by a dark brown rat who alerted us that the king was holding a meeting and everyone better show up or they would be exiled. He then went on his way after smelling the air around us with a questioning face.

We walked into the meeting undetected while the king was in the middle of a speech. He was explaining the importance of not going onto the surface alone, but in small groups. It should have been obvious to everybody but it seemed that some rats weren't that bright. The next thing he spoke of was the topic of 'birds'.

Apparently what I came in contact with the night before was called an owl. The king continued telling us that most birds fed on smaller creatures and had no problem hunting and catching them if their prey was being oblivious.

All of a sudden a horrible squeaking sound echoed in the air and the room went silent. Everyone's head turned to a small white rat that was in the middle row; he'd urinated in the wrong place at the wrong time. As he was pushed forward to address the king, you could hear the terror in his squeaks. When crouching before the king, he apologized profusely. A cold death stare was bestowed upon him by the king who immediately snapped at the albino's leg, jaggedly removing it and throwing the poor rat to the side. The king then walked over and suffocated the rat to death. Our meeting was then adjourned and everyone returned to their beds for the night, except I hid around the corner until everyone had left.

Anger festered inside of me as I walked back into the room to converse with the king. There was no reason to kill any of our kind; we worked hard to find food for everyone while digging to make our home bigger. How dare the king treat us like that? Instead of receiving praise for standing up for everyone, all I received was laughs. In return, I told of a secret I knew of that resided under the king's chamber. I was then humiliated by him as he made sexual and sexist remarks toward me; he didn't believe my secret and that's when I knew things had to change for the better around there.

While scurrying back to my bed, I stopped by and told my friends to wake early the next day for we had a lot of work to do. They asked me what was wrong with working through the night; I had no objection and began leading the way back to the tunnel.

Thankfully, there was no evidence that anyone had ventured near our layout. A couple of hours into digging I noticed that we had no idea how close the town actually was, so I appointed myself to find out. I sculpted a low rise tunnel to the surface; the sunrise beamed down upon my cold face. Town was only half an hour away but our paws became raw from the continuous hours of digging, leaving us with no other choice but to rest until the following night.

We found ourselves digging full force back at the tunnel the following night, all three of us extremely excited. This would be the night we found the market, find the peanut butter, and finally gratify my urge. It was only a short matter of time before we decided to dig our way up to the surface and land us right on the edge of our destination. Emotions got the better of us as we hastily ran behind a random building, not caring what we found.

The air was quiet, not a soul was awake in the small town. Lights flickered inside the windows of the human's homes, leaving the only illumination outside a mix of chilling moonlight and yellow street lights.

We walked across the pavement like we owned the place, while trying to find the closest market, when we were suddenly interrupted by a small creature on four legs. A cat now stood between us. Fortunately, the three of us knew already what we were up against and began to run away as fast as our legs could carry us. The three of us had split up in three different directions, in order to confuse the cat, but now we'd been separated with no way to find each other.

I had to complete the hunt with or without them. They were pretty quick on their feet anyway and would probably end up with me again soon.

Down the street, I saw a small building with a sign in the shape of a bowl of fruit with a dollar sign underneath the crude drawing. As I crossed the street, my body became a silhouette on the right of me. The cat burst into the lights, stopping dead in its tracks as well. In less than a second the cat had been struck by a car. As the vehicle halted above me, I watched as the cat flew more than ten feet in the air to land in the center of the road with a large trail of its bodily fluids in its wake. From where the cat landed, another small body landed as well—the corpse of one of my friends. Two human males exited the car, expressing sounds of anger towards each other. After one male pointed to the dead cat, the other male began to become physical by pushing him around and yelling at him for caring about the cat. Their fight became more intense as one threw the other to the ground, then after kicking him several times, he spat on his bleeding friend's face before returning to the car, leaving the fallen male on the ground. A roaring noise came from above me, then the sound weakened and became louder in succession.

Eventually the car moved forward, rolling over the bodies ahead of it and causing them to empty themselves all over the pavement. Glass shattered around them from a bottle that was thrown from out the car's window. The fallen human remained still.

Sweet and sugary smells were in the breeze. Upon investigating the bodies, I acknowledged that life had left them. Their liquids were slowly mixing together on the pavement and giving off those delicious sweet smells. I was so drawn toward it that I couldn't help but partake in the lovely feast that had presented itself before me. As I fed, I could feel my body warming from the inside. As I guzzled it all down, my eyesight became a little shaky and blurred, and thoughts of being king raced through my head. My legs started to become numb as I stumbled over to the human left on the ground. After sniffing the body, I discerned it was dead. It tasted even more delicious than the cat.

When I could eat no more, I decided the trip to the surface was over and I returned to the lair, and upon finding my bed, fell into a deep sleep.

I awoke in panic, finding myself in a hole where my bed used to be. The walls were splattered with the remaining blood from my lover's skull. The floor was littered in bones and I could feel my fur sticking together all over my back. Again I heard the sounds that had awakened me, the screams of many dying rats. With haste I ran throughout the many tunnels, trying to find what was going on. Black smoke was floating in the air. When I came across the king's chamber, I found a large black rat with several smaller rats attacking and urinating all over the king. It was chaos; most rats couldn't even tell who they were attacking, resulting in an all-out bloodbath. The smoke in the air was thickening; this was the only and safest time for me to escape. While I ran out of the burrows, I met with the most terrifying feelings and sights I'd ever experienced.

I ran straight across the surface, dodging many human hands and dog jaws while trying to block out the sounds of my dying families. Many people had gathered around our home and had stuffed grass and lit torches in our alternate exits in hopes of catching us. It had been told by the previous king that humans might try to harm us if we were found, making it clear to me that it must have been my fault that we'd been found.

Spines were snapped, and necks were slit in the crudest ways. Many of my brethren were repeatedly bashed against the ground until they achieved, hopefully, death, but probably resulted in a lucid coma. Rat fur and skin had begun to litter the ground. Some were being thrown into bags while others were attached with string to poles for easy carrying. I watched from the middle of the field. I watched it all, took it all in, then ran away. I ran as fast as my legs would go. That place was now dead to me; there was no reason to stick around anymore. At that moment it didn't really matter where I ended up, as long as I arrived alive.

I had put a good distance between myself and the town as the sun started to rise. A small wooded area was ahead, the perfect place to take cover.

This is where I met 'T'. After smelling the air around me, I was guided to the center of the woods where a large hill had been formed out of dirt and tree branches. It was inhabited by a small family of sixty. T thought I was a girl; he also thought that if he brought me inside he could mate with me.

Needless to say, there was no way that I would let him onto my secret. Everyone in his family had a name. This was new to me. I'd never thought of naming myself before, so I remained nameless.

I spent several days in the hill, learning about everything the rats did and knew. Many of their names consisted of only single, English alphabet letters, which made it easier for me to remember them all. They weren't very intelligent though, and the only difference between them and my old family were the names. That is, except when I learned that they didn't have a king. My mind was overwhelmed by this. My third task was now in planning, except that this time, all I would need was myself.

It was easy to assemble everyone; they either wanted to have their way with me or just wanted to be my friend. I held a meeting, and as I stood in front of the quiet crowd, I told them of my past life. To become fantastic in their eyes, I began to embellish my stories. So what if I wasn't really an old king, they would never find out, they would only hear the words that were spoken.

Beneath my king's chambers did lay a secret, it was where I learned how to speak and read English, where I learned the names of animals in a sort of secret library. I told them I was a hybrid animal which meant I was both genders; a miracle made just for them. They believed me; they all practically fell in love with me. We were small in size but in large quantities we could do tremendous things. I spoke of how we could be better than the humans and make them afraid of us, but not forgetting to mention how delicious they tasted. Also, I believed I used the words, 'My friends, the warriors' towards them. My stories were immediately eaten up and digested.

For the first time in my life I had the power I always wanted and was ready to abuse it for revenge. Every rat was hanging onto my every word as they blessed me with large quantities of food. I stood atop the pile and thanked every single rat individually by name, and a roar of gratuitous sounds followed. All I had to do was point my nose and they would follow, and that's what I did after revealing my plan to invade the town. Everyone was on board with my plan without the slightest amount of doubt, so at dusk I led them out of the forest.

We ran full speed across the open fields with hopes of not getting eaten by any other wild animals, but it didn't seem to matter because many birds in the sky were on to us. It would have looked odd if one was to look from a distance; several birds had swooped down, attempting to snatch a meal.

We turned it around on them, though, swarming them as they swooped down on us, and leaving a scarce line of bird carcasses from town back to the hill. The sun had begun to set by the time we arrived outside the town. Our group patiently waited in a large patch of tall grass and watched the lights in the windows slowly turn off one by one.

An hour had gone by with us all being silent. As the last light in the furthest home went out, we began to march into town, making sure to hide behind buildings just in case we were seen. I sent a couple of small groups out to scout the windows ahead. Everyone remained undetected; no one was to begin without the rest of us. The stomachs of my warriors began to growl. They became irritated and scared but I reassured them our deeds wouldn't go unjustified. They weren't quite sure what I meant by this, but with their trust in me, others would shame anyone who let them question anything I said.

Eventually we regrouped and were told of many suitable homes that had their windows open, making it easier to enter. After hearing of all the possibilities, I set our sights on a two-story building with a staircase leading to the second floor. Tiny hearts pounded as our feet scurried up the metal staircase. At the top of the stairs was an open window next to a metal door. Everyone gathered at the top, awaiting my next order, and as I climbed up into the window and peered into the room, I found a small female sleeping in her bed. The girl must not have been older than ten years old.

She was the perfect first subject, small, warm, and sleeping. I was silently followed inside by the rest of the group. The room itself smelled delicious, something like cookies and cream with a hint of peach, but it didn't compare to the odors coming from the little girl's hair.

Carefully, everyone found their way onto the bed, outlining the girl's shape. A small whimpering sound came from behind the girl's door, but unfortunately I ignored the warning.

Everything happened so fast after the first bite. It was as if a hurricane had struck the room. The moment I gave the signal, sixty pairs of teeth sank into the girl's warm flesh. She awoke in a panic, falling off the bed and flailing while screaming from the top of her lungs. Small whimpers at the door turned into full-fledged barking and scratching. The rats kept on chewing, trying to ignore the sounds. Her screams became louder and more intense as the rats began to dig holes inside her body, leaving the blood to stream out like she was a faucet.

Then, the door opened.

Our barrage was tackled by a large brown dog, which started to attack and successfully killed several rats with its snapping jaws. The dog was accompanied by a tall man who rushed in and tried to remove the rats from his daughter by smacking them away in a panic. The girl had passed out from blood loss, leading her father to believe that she was already dead.

That's when the shotgun blasts began to blow holes in my warriors and the walls. This was horror for my eyes, pain in my heart, and murder for my ears. The dog's attack had caused me to tumble off the little girl, and everything next felt as if I was stuck in slow motion.

I'd fallen in front of the father and was kicked into the air towards the window. Shots were fired that shattered the glass behind me. I was struck with several pellets that slowly burned their way inside my body while I fell down to the back alley. While I lay in anguish, red and blue lights flashed throughout the town, followed by the loud wail of sirens.

Even the moments that had just happened were flashing with them right before my eyes. I was going to die, there was no doubt about it. Maybe I wasn't fit to be a king after all, but at least I was the rat who had the idea.

Before everything went black for the final time, and my blood seeped out onto the ground beneath me, I wondered what ever happened to my friend with the white spot on his face.

I think if I were to name him, I would have called him *Forte.*

GRAVEYARD RATS

ROBERT E. HOWARD

1
The Head from the Grave

Saul Wilkinson awoke suddenly, and lay in the darkness with beads of cold sweat on his hands and face. He shuddered at the memory of the dream from which he'd awakened.

But horrible dreams were nothing uncommon. Grisly nightmares had haunted his sleep since early childhood. It was another fear that clutched his heart with icy fingers—fear of the sound that had roused him. It had been a furtive step—hands fumbling in the dark.

And now a small scurrying sounded in the room—a rat running back and forth across the floor.

He groped under his pillow with trembling fingers. The house was still, but imagination filled its darkness with shapes of horror. But it wasn't all imagination. A faint stir of air told him the door that led to the broad hallway was open. He knew he'd closed that door before going to bed, and he knew it wasn't one of his brothers who had come so subtly to his room.

In that fear-tense, hate-haunted household, no man came by night to his brother's room without first making himself known.

This was especially the case since an old feud had claimed the eldest brother four days since. John Wilkinson was shot down in the streets of the little hill-country town by Joel Middleton, who had escaped into the post oak grown hills after swearing still greater vengeance against the Wilkinsons.

All this flashed through Saul's mind as he drew the revolver from under his pillow.

As he slid out of bed, the creak of the springs brought his heart into his throat, and he crouched there for a moment, holding his breath and straining his eyes into the darkness.

Richard was sleeping upstairs, and so was Harrison, the city detective Peter had brought out to hunt down Joel Middleton. Peter's room was on the ground floor, but in another wing of the house. A yell for help might awaken all three, but it would also bring a hail of bullets at him if Joel Middleton was crouching across the room in the blackness.

Saul knew this was his fight, and must be fought alone in the darkness he'd always feared and hated. As all this went through his head, that light scampering patter of tiny feet continued, racing up and down, up and down...

Crouching against the wall, cursing the pounding of his heart, Saul fought to steady his quivering nerves. He was backed against the wall which formed the partition between his room and the hallway.

The windows were faint gray squares in the blackness, and he could dimly make out objects of furniture in all except one side of the room. Joel Middleton must be over there, crouching by the old fireplace, which was invisible in the darkness.

But why was he waiting? And why was that accursed rat racing up and down before the fireplace, as if in a frenzy of fear and greed? Saul had seen rats race up and down the floor of the meathouse in the same way, frantic to get at the flesh suspended out of reach.

Noiselessly, Saul moved along the wall toward the door. If a man was in the room, he would presently be lined between himself and a window. But as Saul glided along the wall like a nightshirted ghost, no ominous bulk grew out of the darkness. He reached the door and closed it soundlessly, wincing at his nearness to the unrelieved blackness of the hall outside.

But nothing happened. The only sounds were the wild beating of his heart, the loud ticking of the old clock on the mantelpiece, and the maddening patter of the unseen rat. Saul clenched his teeth against the shrieking of his tortured nerves. Even in his growing terror he found time to wonder frantically why that rat was running up and down before the fireplace.

The tension became unbearable. The open door proved that Middleton, someone—or something—had come into the room. Why would Middleton come except to kill? But why in God's name had he not struck already? What was he waiting for?

Saul's nerve suddenly snapped. The darkness was strangling him and those pattering rat-feet were red-hot hammers on his crumbling brain. He must have light, even though that light brought hot lead ripping through him.

In stumbling haste he groped to the mantelpiece, fumbling for the lamp. He cried out—a choked, horrible croak that couldn't have carried beyond his room. For his hand, groping in the dark on the mantel, had touched the hair on a human scalp!

A furious squeal sounded in the darkness at his feet and a sharp pain pierced his ankle as the rat attacked him, as if he were an intruder seeking to rob it of some coveted object.

But Saul was hardly aware of the rodent as he kicked it away and reeled back, his brain a whirling turmoil. Matches and candles were on the table, and to them he lurched, his hands sweeping the dark and finding what he wanted.

He lit a candle and turned, gun lifted in a shaking hand. There was no living man in the room except himself. But his distended eyes focused themselves on the mantelpiece…and the object on it.

He stood frozen, his mind at first refusing to register what his eyes revealed. Then he croaked inhumanly and the gun fell onto the hearth as it slipped through his numb fingers.

John Wilkinson was dead with a bullet through his heart. It had been three days since Saul had seen his body nailed into the crude coffin and lowered into the grave in the old Wilkinson family graveyard. For three days the hard clay soil had baked in the hot sun above the coffined form of John Wilkinson.

Yet from the mantel, John Wilkinson's face leered at him—white and cold and dead. It was no nightmare, no dream of madness. There on the mantelpiece, rested John Wilkinson's severed head.

And before the fireplace, up and down, up and down, scampered a creature with red eyes that squeaked and squealed—a great gray rat, maddened by its failure to reach the flesh its ghoulish hunger craved.

Saul Wilkinson began to laugh— horrible, soul-shaking shrieks that mingled with the squealing of the gray rat. Saul's body rocked back and forth. Then the laughter turned to insane weeping that gave way in turn to hideous screams that echoed through the old house and roused the other sleepers.

They were the screams of a madman. The horror of what he'd seen had blasted Saul Wilkinson's reason like a blown-out candle flame.

2

Madman's Hate

It was those screams which roused Steve Harrison, sleeping in an upstairs room. Before he was fully awake he was on his way down the unlighted stairs, a pistol in one hand and a flashlight in the other.

Down in the hallway he saw light streaming from under a closed door and made for it. But another was before him. Just as Harrison reached the landing, he saw a figure rushing across the hall, and flashed his light beam on it.

It was Peter Wilkinson, tall and gaunt, with a fire poker in his hand. He yelled something incoherent, threw open the door, and rushed in.

Harrison heard him exclaim, "Saul! What's the matter? What are you looking at?" Then a terrible cry of, "My God!"

The poker clanged on the floor, and then the screams of the maniac rose to a crescendo of fury. It was at this instant that Harrison reached the door and took in the scene with one startled glance. He saw two men in nightshirts grappling in the candlelight, while from the mantel a cold, dead, white face looked blindly down on them, and a gray rat ran in mad circles around their feet.

Into that scene of horror and madness Harrison propelled his powerful, thick-set body. Peter Wilkinson was in sore straits. He'd dropped his poker and now, with blood streaming from a wound on his head, was vainly striving to tear Saul's lean fingers from his throat.

The glare in Saul's eyes told Harrison that the man was mad. Crooking one massive arm around the maniac's neck, he tore him loose from his victim with an exertion of sheer strength that not even the abnormal energy of insanity could resist.

The madman's stringy muscles were like steel wires under the detective's hands, and Saul twisted about in Harrison's grasp, his teeth snapping, beastlike, for the detective's bull-throat. Harrison shoved the clawing, frothing fury away from him and smashed a fist at the madman's jaw. Saul crashed to the floor and lay still, eyes glazed and limbs quivering.

Peter reeled back against a table, purple-faced and gagging.

"Get something to tie him with, quick!" Harrison snapped, heaving the limp figure off the floor and letting it slump into a great arm-chair. "Here, tear that sheet into strips. We've got to secure him before he comes to. Hell's fire!"

The rat had made a ravening attack on the senseless man's bare feet. Harrison kicked it away, but it squeaked furiously and came charging back with ghoulish persistence. Harrison crushed it under his foot, cutting short its maddened squeal.

Peter, gasping convulsively, thrust into the detective's hands the strips he'd torn from the sheet, and Harrison bound Saul's limp limbs with professional efficiency. In the midst of his task he looked up to see Richard, the youngest brother, standing in the doorway, his face like chalk.

"Richard!" Peter choked. "Look! My God! John's head!"

"I see!" Richard licked his lips. "But why are you tying up Saul?"

"He's crazy," Harrison snapped. "Get me some whiskey, will you?"

As Richard reached for a bottle on a curtained shelf, booted feet hit the porch outside, and a voice yelled, "Hey, there, Richard! What's wrong?"

"That's our neighbor, Jim Allison," Peter muttered. He stepped to the door opposite the one that opened into the hall and turned the key in the ancient lock. The door opened onto a side porch.

A tousle-headed man with his pants pulled on over his night-shirt came blundering in. "What's the matter?" he demanded. "I heard somebody hollerin', and I ran over quick as I could. What're you doin' to Saul—good God Almighty!" He'd seen the head on the mantel and his face went ashen.

"Go get the marshal, Jim!" Peter croaked. "This is Joel Middle-ton's work!"

Jim Allison hurried out, stumbling as he peered back over his shoulder in morbid fascination.

Harrison had managed to spill some liquor between Saul's livid lips. He handed the bottle to Peter and stepped to the mantel. He touched the grisly object, shivering slightly as he did so. His eyes narrowed suddenly. "You think Middleton dug up your brother's grave and cut off his head?" he asked.

"Who else?" Peter stared blankly at him.

"Saul's mad. Madmen do strange things. Maybe Saul did this."

"No! No!" Peter exclaimed, shuddering. "Saul hasn't left the house all day. John's grave was undisturbed this morning when I stopped by the old graveyard on my way to the farm. Saul was sane when he went to bed. It was seeing John's head that drove him mad. Joel Middleton's been here to take this horrible revenge!" He sprang up suddenly, shrilling, "My God, he may still be hiding in the house somewhere!"

"We'll search it," Harrison said. "Richard, you stay here with Saul. Peter, you come with me."

In the hall outside, the detective directed a beam of light on the heavy front door. The key was turned in the massive lock so the door was still secure. No one had entered that way. He turned and strode down the hall. "Which door is farthest from any sleeping chamber?" he asked.

"The back kitchen door!" Peter answered and led the way. A few moments later they were standing before it. It stood partly open, framing a crack of starlit sky.

"He must have come and gone this way," Harrison muttered. "You're sure this door was locked?"

"I locked all the outer doors myself before bed," Peter asserted. "Look at those scratches on the outer side! And there's the key lying on the floor inside."

"Old-fashioned lock," Harrison grunted. "A man could work the key out with a wire from the outer side and force the lock easily. This is the logical lock to force, too, because the noise of breaking it wouldn't likely be heard by anyone in the house." He stepped out onto the back porch. The broad backyard was without trees or bushes, separated by a barbed-wire fence from a pasture lot, which ran to a wood-lot thickly grown with post oaks, which was part of the woods which hemmed in the village of Lost Knob on all sides.

Peter stared toward that woodland, a low, black rampart in the faint starlight. He shivered. "He's out there, somewhere," he whispered. "I never suspected he'd dare strike at us in our own house. I brought you here to hunt him down. I never thought we'd need you to protect us!"

Without replying, Harrison stepped down into the yard. Peter cringed back from the starlight, and remained crouching at the edge of the porch.

Harrison crossed the narrow pasture and paused at the ancient rail fence which separated it from the woods. They were black as only post oak thickets could be. No rustle of leaves, no scrape of branches betrayed a lurking presence. If Joel Middleton had been there, he'd already sought refuge in the rugged hills that surrounded Lost Knob.

Harrison turned back toward the house. He'd arrived at Lost Knob late the preceding evening. It was now past midnight, but the grisly news was spreading, even in the dead of night.

The Wilkinson house stood at the western edge of the town, and the Allison house was the only one within a hundred yards of it, but Harrison saw lights springing up in distant windows.

Peter stood on the porch, head out-thrust on his long, buzzard-like neck. "Find anything?" he called anxiously.

"Tracks wouldn't show on this hard-baked ground," the detective grunted. "Just what did you see when you ran into Saul's room?"

"Saul standing before the mantel, screaming with his mouth wide open," Peter answered. "When I saw what he saw, I must have cried out and dropped the poker. Then Saul leaped on me like a wild beast."

"Was his door locked?"

"Closed, but not locked. The lock got broken accidentally a few days ago."

"One more question: has Middleton ever been in this house before?" Harrison asked.

"Not to my knowledge," Peter replied grimly. "Our families have hated each other for twenty-five years. Joel's the last of his name."

Harrison re-entered the house. Jim Allison had returned with Marshal McVey, a tall taciturn man who plainly resented the detective's presence. Men were gathering on the side porch and in the yard. They talked in low mutters, except for Jim Allison, who was vociferous in his indignation.

"This finishes Joel Middleton!" Allison proclaimed loudly. "Some folks sided with him when he killed John. I wonder what they think now? Diggin' up a dead man and cuttin' his head off! That's Injun work! I reckon folks won't wait for no jury to tell 'em what to do with Joel Middleton!"

"Better catch him before you start lynchin' him," McVey grunted. "Peter, I'm takin' Saul to the county seat."

Peter nodded mutely. Saul was recovering consciousness, but the mad glaze of his eyes was unaltered.

Harrison said, "Suppose we go to the Wilkinson graveyard and see what we can find? We might be able to track Middleton from there."

"They brought you here to do the job they didn't think I was good enough to do," McVey snarled. "All right. Go 'head and do it—alone. I'm takin' Saul to the county seat." With the aid of his deputies, he lifted the bound maniac and strode out of the house. Neither Peter nor Richard offered to accompany him.

A tall, gangly man stepped from among his fellows and awkwardly addressed Harrison. "What the marshal does is his own business, but all of us here are ready to help all we can, if you want to get a posse together and comb the country for Middleton."

"Thanks, but no." Harrison was unintentionally abrupt. "You can help me by all clearing out, right now. I'll work this thing out alone, in my own way, as the marshal suggested."

The men moved off at once, silent and resentful, and Jim Allison followed them after a moment's hesitation. When all had gone, Harrison closed the door and turned to Peter. "Will you take me to the graveyard?" he asked.

Peter shuddered. "Isn't it a terrible risk? Middleton has shown he'll stop at nothing."

"Why should he?" Richard laughed savagely. His jaw was taut, his eyes alive with harsh mockery, and lines of suffering were carven deep in his face. "We never stopped hounding him," Richard added. "John cheated him out of his last bit of land—that's why Middleton killed him. For which you were devoutly thankful!"

"You're talking wild!" Peter exclaimed.

Richard laughed bitterly. "You old hypocrite! We're all beasts of prey, we Wilkinsons—like this thing!" He kicked the dead rat viciously. "We all hated each other. You're glad Saul's crazy! You're glad John's dead. Only I'm left now, and I have a heart disease. Oh, stare if you like! I'm no fool. I've seen you poring over Aaron's lines in 'Titus Andronicus.' 'Oft have I digg'd up dead men from their graves, and set them upright at their dear friends' doors!' "

"You're mad yourself, Richard!" Peter sprang up, livid.

"Oh, am I?" Richard had lashed himself almost into a frenzy. "What proof have we that you didn't cut off John's head? You knew Saul was a neurotic, that a shock like that might drive him insane! You visited the graveyard yesterday, too!"

Peter's contorted face was a mask of fury. Then, with an effort of iron control, he relaxed and said quietly, "You're over-wrought, Richard."

"Saul and John hated you," Richard snarled. "I know why. It was because you wouldn't agree to leasing our farm on Wild River to that oil company. If not for your stubbornness we might all be wealthy."

"You know why I wouldn't lease," Peter snapped. "Drilling there would ruin the agricultural value of the land—certain profit, not a risky gamble like oil."

"So you say," Richard sneered. "But suppose that's just a smoke screen? Suppose you dream of being the sole-surviving heir, and becoming an oil millionaire all by yourself, with no brothers to share it with."

Harrison broke in, "Are we going the chew the rag all night?"

"No!" Peter turned his back on his brother. "I'll take you to the graveyard. I'd rather face Joel Middleton in the night than listen to the ravings of this lunatic any longer."

"I'm not going," Richard snarled. "Out there in the black night there's too many chances for you to remove the remaining heir. I'll stay the rest of the night with Jim Allison." He opened the door and vanished in the darkness.

Peter picked up the severed head and wrapped it in a cloth, shivering lightly as he did so. "Did you notice how well preserved the face is?" he muttered. "One would think that after three days…" he paused. "I'll take it and put it back in the grave where it belongs."

"I'll kick the dead rat outside," Harrison began, turning, and then stopped short. "The damned thing's gone!"

Peter Wilkinson paled as his eyes swept the empty floor. "It was there!" he whispered. "It was dead. You smashed it! It couldn't have come to life and run away."

"Well, what about it?" Harrison didn't mean to waste time on this minor mystery.

Peter's eyes gleamed wearily in the candlelight. "It was a graveyard rat," he whispered. "I never saw one in an inhabited house, or in town before! The Indians used to tell strange tales about them! They said they weren't rats at all, but evil, cannibal demons into which entered the spirits of wicked, dead men at whose corpses they gnawed!"

"Hell's fire!" Harrison snorted, blowing out the candle. His flesh crawled. After all, a dead rat couldn't crawl away by itself.

3

The Feathered Shadow

Clouds had rolled across the stars. The air was hot and sti-fling. The narrow, rutty road that wound westward into the hills was atrocious. Despite this, Peter Wilkinson handled his ancient Model T Ford skillfully, and the town was quickly lost to sight behind them. They passed no more houses. On each side the dense post oak thickets crowded close to the barbed-wire fences.

Peter broke the silence suddenly. "How did that rat come into our house? They overrun the woods along the creeks, and swarm in every country graveyard in the hills, but I never saw one in town before. It must have followed Joel Middleton when he brought the head."

A lurch and a monotonous bumping brought a curse from Harrison. The car came to a stop with a grinding of brakes.

"Flat," Peter muttered. "Won't take me long to change tires. You watch the woods. Joel Middleton might be hiding anywhere."

That seemed good advice. While Peter wrestled with rusty metal and stubborn rubber, Harrison stood between him and the nearest clump of trees with his hand on his revolver. The night wind blew fitfully through the leaves, and once he thought he caught the gleam of tiny eyes among the stems.

"That's got it," Peter announced at last, turning to let down the jack. "We've wasted enough time."

"Listen!" Harrison said in a tense voice.

Off to the west sounded a sudden scream of pain or fear, then came the impact of racing feet on the hard ground and the crackling of brush, as if someone was fleeing blindly through the bushes within a few hundred yards of the road. In an instant Harrison was over the fence and running toward the sounds.

"Help! Help!" It was the voice of dire terror. "Almighty God! Help me!"

"This way!" Harrison yelled, bursting into an open area. The unseen fugitive evidently altered his course in response, for the heavy footfalls grew louder, and then there rang out a terrible shriek as a figure staggered from the bushes on the opposite side of the glade and fell headlong.

The dim starlight showed a vague writhing shape, with a darker figure on its back. Harrison caught the glint of steel and heard the sound of a blow.

He brought up his gun and fired. At the crack of the shot, the darker figure rolled free, leaped up, and vanished in the bushes. Harrison ran on, a chill crawling along his spine because of what he'd seen in the flash of the shot.

He crouched at the edge of the bushes and peered into them. The shadowy figure had come and gone, leaving no trace except the man who lay groaning in the glade.

Harrison bent over him, snapping on his flashlight. He was an old man, a wild, unkempt figure with matted white hair and beard. That beard was stained with red now, and blood oozed from a deep stab wound in his back.

"Who did this?" Harrison demanded, seeing that it was useless to try to stanch the flow of blood. The old man was dying. "Joel Middleton?"

"It couldn't have been!" Peter had followed the detective. "That's old Josh Sullivan, a friend of Joel's. He's half crazy, but I've suspected that he's been keeping in touch with Joel and giving him tips."

"Joel Middleton," the old man muttered. "I'd been out to find him, to tell him the news about John's head."

"Where's Joel hiding?" the detective demanded.

Sullivan choked on a flow of blood, then spat and shook his head. "You'll never learn it from me!" He turned his gaze on Peter with the eerie glare of the dying. "Are you taking your brother's head back to his grave, Peter Wilkinson? Be careful you don't find your own grave before this night's done! Evil on all your name! The devil owns your souls and the graveyard rats'll eat your flesh! The ghost of the dead walks the night!"

"What do you mean?" Harrison demanded. "Who stabbed you?"

"A dead man!" Sullivan was going fast. "As I come back from meetin' Joel Middleton I met him. Wolf Hunter, the Tonkawa chief your grandpap murdered so long ago, Peter Wilkinson! He chased me and knifed me. I saw him plain in the starlight—naked in his loin-cloth and feathers and paint, just as I saw him when I was a child, before your grandpap killed him! Wolf Hunter took your brother's head from the grave!" Sullivan's voice was a ghastly whisper. "He's come back from Hell to fulfill the curse he laid on your grandpa when your grandpap shot him in the back to get the land his tribe claimed. Beware! His ghost walks the night! The graveyard rats are his servants. The graveyard rats…" Blood burst from his white-bearded lips and he sank back, dead.

Harrison rose somberly. "Let him lie here. We'll pick up his body as we go back to town. We're going on to the graveyard."

"Dare we?" Peter's face was white. "A human I don't fear, not even Joel Middleton, but a ghost…"

"Don't be a fool!" Harrison snorted. "Didn't you say the old man was half crazy?"

"But what if Joel Middleton is hiding somewhere near?"

"I'll take care of him!" Harrison had an invincible confidence in his own fighting ability. What he didn't tell Peter, as they returned to the car, was that he'd had a glimpse of the killer in the flash of his gunshot. The memory of that glimpse still had the short hairs prickling at the base of his skull. The figure had been naked but for a loin-cloth, moccasins and a headdress of feathers.

"Who was Wolf Hunter?" Harrison asked after they'd returned to the car and drove on.

"A Tonkawa chief," Peter replied. "He befriended my grandfather and was later murdered by him, just as Josh said. They say his bones lie in the old graveyard to this day." Peter lapsed into silence, seemingly prey of morbid broodings.

Some four miles from town the road wound past a dim clearing. The Wilkinson graveyard was located there. A rusty barbed-wire fence surrounded a cluster of graves, the white, moss-covered headstones leaning at crazy angles. Weeds grew thick, straggling over the low mounds.

The post oaks crowded close on all sides, and the road wound through them, past the sagging gate. Across the tops of the trees, nearly half a mile to the west, there was visible a shapeless bulk which Harrison knew was the roof of a house.

"The old Wilkinson farmhouse," Peter said, as if he'd read Harrison's thoughts. "I was born there; so were my brothers.

Nobody's lived in it since we moved to town ten years ago." He pulled over and parked the vehicle, the two men getting out.

Peter's nerves were taut. He glanced fearfully at the black woods around him, and his hands trembled as he lighted a lantern taken from the car. He winced as he picked up the round cloth-wrapped object that lay on the back seat; perhaps he was visualizing the cold, white, stony face that cloth concealed.

As Peter climbed over the low gate and led the way between the weed-grown mounds, he said, "We're fools. If Joel Middleton's lying out there in the woods he could pick us both off as easy as shooting rabbits."

Harrison didn't reply, and a moment later Peter halted and shone the light on a mound which was bare of weeds. The surface was tumbled and disturbed.

"Look!" Peter exclaimed. "I expected to find an open grave. Why do you think he took the trouble to fill it in again?"

"We'll see," Harrison grunted. "Are you game to open that grave?"

"I've seen my brother's head," Peter answered grimly. "I think I'm man enough to look on his headless body without fainting. There are tools in the tool-shed by the corner of the fence. I'll get them."

Returning presently with pick and shovel, he set the lighted lantern on the ground, and the cloth-wrapped head near it. Peter was pale, and sweat stood on his brow in thick drops. The lantern cast their shadows, grotesquely distorted, across the weed-grown graves. The air was oppressive. There was an occasional dull flicker of lightning along the dusky horizons.

"What's that?" Harrison paused, pick lifted. All about them sounded rustling and scurrying among the weeds. Beyond the circle of lantern light clusters of tiny red beads glittered at the two men.

"Rats!" Peter hurled a stone and the beads vanished, though the rustlings grew louder. "They swarm in this graveyard. I believe they'd devour a living man if they caught him helpless. Begone, you servants of Satan!"

Harrison took the shovel and began scooping out mounds of loose dirt.

"Shouldn't be hard work," he grunted. "If he dug it out today or early tonight, this dirt'll be loose all the way down." With a prickling in the short hairs at the nape of his neck, he stopped short with his shovel jammed hard in the dirt. In the tense silence he heard the graveyard rats running through the grass.

"What's the matter?" A new pallor grayed Peter's face.

"I've hit solid ground," Harrison said slowly. "In three days after being disturbed this clay soil would be baked hard as a brick. But if Middleton or anybody else had opened this grave and refilled it today, the soil would be loose all the way down. It's not. Below the first few inches it's packed and baked hard! The top has been scratched, but the grave has never been opened since it was first filled three days ago!"

Peter staggered. "Then it's true!" he screamed. "Wolf Hunter has come back! He reached up from Hell and took John's head without opening the grave! He sent his familiar devil into our house in the form of a rat! A ghost-rat that couldn't be killed!" Harrison tried to grab Peter who cried out, "Hands off, curse you!"

"Damn it, pull yourself together, Peter!" Harrison growled.

Peter struck Harrison's arm aside and tore free. He turned and ran—not toward the car parked outside the graveyard, but toward the opposite fence. He scrambled across the rusty wires with a ripping of cloth and vanished into the woods, heedless of Harrison's shouts.

"Hell!" Harrison pulled up from chasing Peter and swore more fervently. Where but in the black hill country could such things happen? Angrily he picked up the tools and dug into the close-packed clay that was baked by a blazing sun into almost iron hardness. Sweat rolled from him in streams, and he grunted and swore, but persevered with all the power of his massive muscles. He meant to prove or disprove a suspicion growing in his mind—a suspicion that the body of John Wilkinson had never been placed in that grave.

The lightning flashed often and closer, and a low booming of thunder began in the west. An occasional gust of wind made the lantern flicker, and as the mound beside the grave grew higher, and the man digging sank lower and lower into the earth, the rustling in the grass grew louder, the red beads beginning to glint in the weeds. Harrison heard the eerie gnashing of tiny teeth all about him, and swore at the memory of grisly legends whispered by the old black women of his boyhood region about the grave-yard rats.

The grave wasn't deep. No Wilkinson would waste much labor on the dead. At last the crude coffin lay uncovered before him. With the point of the pick he pried up one corner of the lid and held the lantern close to peer inside the coffin. A startled oath escaped his lips. The coffin wasn't empty. It held a huddled, headless figure.

Harrison climbed out of the grave, his mind racing to fit to-gether pieces of the puzzle. The stray bits snapped into place, forming a pattern, dim and yet incomplete, but taking shape. He looked for the cloth-wrapped head, and got a frightful shock.

The head was gone!

For an instant Harrison felt cold sweat clammy on his hands. Then he heard a clamorous squeaking and the gnashing of tiny fangs.

He caught up the lantern and shone the light about him. In its reflection he saw a white blotch on the grass near a straggling clump of bushes that had invaded the clearing. It was the cloth in which the head had been wrapped. Beyond that a black, squirming mound heaved and tumbled with nauseous life.

With an oath of horror he leaped forward, striking and kicking. The graveyard rats abandoned the head with rasping squeaks, scattering before him like darting black shadows. Harrison shuddered, for it was no face that stared up at him in the lantern light, but a white, grinning skull, to which clung only shreds of gnawed flesh.

While the detective had been digging into John Wilkinson's grave, the graveyard rats had been busy tearing the flesh from the dead man's severed head.

Harrison stooped and picked up the hideous thing, now triply hideous. He wrapped it in the cloth, and as he straightened, something like fright took hold of him. He was ringed in on all sides by a solid circle of gleaming red sparks that shone from the grass. Held back by their fear, the graveyard rats surrounded him, squealing their hate.

Demons, the blacks called them, and in that moment Harrison was ready to agree. The rats gave back before him as he turned toward the grave, and he didn't see the dark figure that slunk from the bushes behind him. Thunder boomed out overhead, drowning even the squeaking of the rats, but he heard the swift footfall behind him an instant before the blow was struck.

He whirled, drawing his gun and dropping the head, but just as he turned, something like a louder clap of thunder exploded in his head, a shower of sparks appearing before his eyes.

As Harrison reeled backward, he fired blindly and cried out as the flash showed him a horrific, half-naked, painted, feathered figure, crouching with a tomahawk uplifted—the open grave was behind Harrison as he fell.

Down into the grave he toppled, his head striking the edge of the coffin with a sickening impact. His powerful body went limp, and like darting shadows, from every side raced the graveyard rats, hurling themselves into the grave in a frenzy of hunger and blood-lust.

4

Rats in Hell

It seemed to Harrison's stunned brain that he lay in blackness on the darkened floors of Hell, a blackness lit by darts of flame from the eternal fires. The triumphant shrieking of demons was in his ears as they stabbed him with red-hot skewers.

He saw them, now—dancing monstrosities with pointed noses, twitching ears, red eyes and gleaming teeth. A sharp pain knifed through his flesh.

Then suddenly the mists cleared and he lay not on the floor of Hell, but on a coffin in the bottom of a grave. The fires were lightning flashes from the black sky, and the demons were rats that swarmed over him, slashing with razor-sharp teeth.

Harrison yelled and heaved convulsively, and at his movement the rats gave back in alarm. But they didn't leave the grave; they massed solidly along the walls, their eyes glittering red.

Harrison knew he could have been senseless only a few seconds. Otherwise, the gray ghouls would have already stripped the living flesh from his bones, as they had ripped the dead flesh from the head of the man on whose coffin he lay.

Already his body was stinging in a score of places and his clothing was damp with his own blood. Cursing, he started to rise, as a chill of panic shot through him. Upon falling, his left arm had become jammed into the partly-open coffin, and the weight of his body on the lid had clamped his hand fast. Harrison fought down a mad wave of terror.

He wouldn't withdraw his hand unless he could lift his body from the coffin lid, and the imprisonment of his hand held him prostrate there.

He was trapped!

In a murdered man's grave, no less, with his hand locked in the coffin of a headless corpse, with a thousand gray ghoul-rats ready to tear the flesh from his living frame!

As if sensing his helplessness, the rats swarmed upon him. Harrison fought for his life, like a man in a nightmare. He kicked, he yelled, he cursed, he smote them with the heavy six-shooter he still clutched in his hand.

Their fangs tore at him, ripping cloth and flesh, their acrid scent nauseated him; they almost covered him with their squirming, writhing bodies. He beat them back, smashed and crushed them with the blows of his six-shooter barrel.

The rodents fell on their dead brothers, cannibalizing their brethren. In desperation Harrison twisted half-over and jammed the muzzle of his gun against the coffin lid. At the flash of fire and the deafening report, the rats scurried away in all directions.

Again and again he pulled the trigger until the gun was empty. The heavy slugs crashed through the lid, splitting off a great sliver from the edge. Harrison drew his bruised hand from the aperture, and gagging and shaking, he clambered out of the grave and rose groggily to his feet. Blood was clotted in his hair from the gash the ghostly hatchet had made in his scalp, and blood trickled from a score of tiny tooth-wounds in his flesh.

Lightning played constantly, but the lantern was still shining. But it wasn't on the ground. It seemed to be suspended in mid-air. Then he was aware that it was held in the hand of a man, a tall man in a black slicker, whose eyes burned dangerously under his broad hat-brim. In his other hand a black pistol muzzle menaced the detective's midriff.

"You must be that damn low-country lawman Pete Wilkinson brung up here to run me down!" growled the man.

"You must be Joel Middleton," Harrison grunted.

"Sure I am!" the outlaw snarled. "Where's Pete, the old devil?"

"He got scared and ran off."

"Crazy, like Saul maybe," Middleton sneered. "Well, you tell him I been savin' a slug for his ugly mug a long time. One for Richard, too."

"Why did you come here?" Harrison demanded.

"I heard shootin'. I got here just as you was climbin' out of the grave. What's the matter with you? Who was it that broke your head?"

"I don't know his name," Harrison answered, caressing his aching head.

"Well, it don't make no difference to me. But I want to tell you that I didn't cut John's head off. I killed him because he needed it." The outlaw swore and spat. "But I didn't do that other deed!"

"I know you didn't," Harrison said.

"Eh?" The outlaw was obviously startled.

"Do you know which rooms the Wilkinsons sleep in at their house in town?"

"Naw," Middleton snorted. "Never was in their house in my life."

"I thought not. Whoever put John's head on Saul's mantel knew. The back kitchen door was the only one where the lock could have been forced without waking somebody up. The lock on Saul's door was broken. You couldn't have known those things. It looked like an inside job from the start. The lock was forced to make it look like an outside job."

Richard spilled some stuff that cinched my belief that it was Peter. I decided to bring him out to the graveyard and see if his nerve would stand up under an accusation across his brother's open coffin. But I hit hard-packed soil and knew the grave hadn't been opened. It gave me a turn and I blurted out what I'd found. But it's simple, after all.

"Peter wanted to get rid of his brothers. When you killed John, that suggested a way to dispose of Saul. John's body was in its coffin in the Wilkinsons' parlor until it was placed in the grave the next day. No death watch was kept. It was easy for Peter to go into the parlor while his brothers slept, pry up the coffin lid and cut off John's head. He put it on ice somewhere to preserve it. When I touched it I found it was nearly frozen.

"No one knew what had happened, because the coffin wasn't opened again. John was an atheist, and there was the briefest sort of ceremony. The coffin wasn't opened for his friends to take a last look, as is the usual custom. Then tonight the head was placed in Saul's room and it drove him insane.

"I don't know why Peter waited until tonight, or why he called me into the case. He must be partly insane himself. I don't think he meant to kill me when we drove out here tonight. But when he discovered I knew the grave hadn't been opened tonight, he saw the game was up. I should have been smart enough to keep my mouth shut, but I was so sure that Peter had opened the grave to get the head, that when I found it hadn't been opened I spoke involuntarily, without stopping to think of the other alternative. Peter pretended a panic and ran off. Later he sent back his partner to kill me."

"Who's that?" Middleton asked.

"How should I know? Some fellow who looks like an Indian!"

"Sounds to me like that old yarn about a Tonkawa ghost has gone to your brain!" Middleton scoffed.

"I didn't say it was a ghost," Harrison said, nettled. "It was real enough to kill your friend Josh Sullivan!"

"What?" Middleton yelled. "Josh got killed? Who done it?"

"The Tonkawa ghost, whoever he is. The body is lying about a mile back beside the road, amongst the thickets, if you don't believe me."

Middleton let out a terrible oath. "By God, I'll kill somebody for that! Stay where you are! I ain't goin' to shoot no unarmed man, but if you try to run me down I'll kill you sure as Hell. So keep off my trail. I'm goin', and don't you try to follow me!" The next instant Middleton had dashed the lantern to the ground where it went out with a clatter of breaking glass.

Harrison blinked in the sudden darkness that followed, and the next lightning flash showed him standing alone in the ancient graveyard. The outlaw was gone.

5

The Rats Eat

Cursing, Harrison groped on the ground which was lit by the lightning flashes. Though he found the broken lantern, he found something else as well.

Rain drops splashed against his face as he started toward the gate. One instant he stumbled in velvet blackness, the next the tombstones shone white in the dazzling glare of the lightning. Harrison's head ached frightfully. Only luck and a tough skull had saved his life. The would-be killer must have thought the blow was fatal and fled, taking John Wilkinson's head with him for what grisly purpose there was no knowing.

Harrison winced at the thought of the rain filling the open grave, but he had neither the strength nor the inclination to shovel the dirt back in it. To remain in that dark graveyard might well mean his death. The killer might return.

129

Harrison looked back as he climbed the fence. The rain had disturbed the rats and the weeds were alive with scampering, flame-eyed shadows. With a shudder, Harrison made his way to the car. He climbed in, found his flashlight and reloaded his revolver.

The rain grew in volume. Soon the rutty road to Lost Knob would be a welter of mud. In his condition he didn't feel able to the task of driving back through the storm over that abominable road, but it couldn't be long until dawn. He decided the old farmhouse would afford him a refuge until daylight.

The rain came down in sheets, soaking him, dimming the already uncertain lights as he drove along the road, splashing noisily through the mud puddles. Wind ripped through the post oaks. Once he grunted and batted his eyes. He could have sworn that a flash of lightning had fleetingly revealed a painted, naked, feathered figure gliding among the trees!

The road wound up to a thickly wooded structure, rising close to the bank of a muddy creek. On the summit the old house squatted. Weeds and low bushes from the surrounding woods were growing right up to the sagging porch. Harrison parked the car as close to the house as possible, and climbed out, struggling with the wind and rain.

He expected to have to blow the lock off the door with his gun, but the door opened easily. He stumbled into a musty-smelling room, weirdly lit by the flickering of the lightning through the cracks of the shutters.

His flashlight revealed a rude bunk built against a side wall, a heavy hand-hewn table, and a pile of rags in a corner. From this pile of rags black furtive shadows darted in all directions.

Rats! Rats again! Could he never escape them?

He closed the door and lit the lantern, placing it on the table. The broken chimney caused the flame to dance and flicker, but not enough wind found its way into the room to blow it out. Three doors, leading into the interior of the house, were closed. The floor and walls were pitted with holes gnawed by the rats. Tiny red eyes glared at him from the apertures.

Harrison sat down on the bunk, the flashlight and pistol on his lap. He expected to have to fight for his life before day broke. Peter Wilkinson was out there in the storm somewhere, with a heart full of murder, and either allied to him or working separately—in either case an enemy to Harrison—was the mysterious painted figure. And that figure was Death, whether as a living masquerader or an Indian ghost.

In any event, the shutters would protect him from a gunshot from the dark, and to get at him his enemies would have to come into the lighted room where he would have an even chance— which was all the big detective had ever asked.

To get his mind off the ghoulish red eyes glaring at him from the floor, Harrison brought out the object that he'd found lying near the broken lantern, where his attacker must have dropped it.

It was a smooth oval of flint, made fast to a handle with rawhide thongs—the Indian tomahawk of an elder generation. Harrison's eyes narrowed suddenly for there was blood on the flint, and some of it was his own. But on the other point of the oval there was more blood, dark and crusted, with strands of hair lighter than his clinging to the clotted point.

Josh Sullivan's blood? No. The old man had been knifed. But someone else had died this night. The darkness had hidden another grim deed.

Black shadows were stealing across the floor. The rats were coming back; ghoulish shapes, creeping from their holes, converging on the pile of rags in the far corner, which on closer investigation was really a tattered carpet rolled into a long, compact heap. Why should the rats leap on that rag? Why should they race up and down along it, squealing and biting at the fabric?

There was something hideously suggestive about its contour, a shape that grew more definite and ghastly as he continued to look. The rats scattered, squeaking loudly, as Harrison sprang across the room. He tore away the carpet, -and looked down on the corpse of Peter Wilkinson.

The back of his head had been crushed and the white face was twisted in a leer of awful terror. For an instant Harrison's brain reeled with the ghastly possibilities his discovery summoned up. Then he took a firm grasp on himself, fought off the whispering potency of the dark, howling night, the thrashing wet black woods and the abysmal aura of the ancient hills, and recognized the only sane solution of the riddle.

Somberly he looked down on the dead man. Peter Wilkinson's fright had been genuine, after all. In his blind panic he'd reverted to the habits of his boyhood and fled toward his old home—and met death instead of security.

Harrison looked up, startled as a weird sound smote his ears above the roar of the storm--the wailing horror of an Indian war-whoop. The killer was upon him!

Harrison dashed over to a shuttered window and peered through a crack, waiting for a flash of lightning. When it came he fired through the window at a feathered head he saw looking around a tree close to the car.

In the darkness that followed the flash Harrison crouched down, waiting. Then there came another white glare and he grunted explosively but didn't fire. The head was still there and he was able to get a better look at it. The lightning shone weirdly white upon it.

It was John Wilkinson's fleshless skull, clad in a feathered headdress and bound in place—it was the bait of a trap.

Harrison wheeled and sprang toward the lantern on the table. That grisly ruse had been to draw his attention to the front of the house while the killer crept up on him through the rear of the house! The rats squealed and scattered before him. Even as Harrison whirled, an inner door began to open. He fired his gun, sending a heavy slug through the panel of the door. A moment later he heard a groan and the sound of a falling body, and then, just as he reached a hand to extinguish the lantern, the world crashed over his head.

A blinding burst of lightning, a deafening clap of thunder, and the ancient house staggered from gables to its foundations. Blue fire crackled from the ceiling and ran down the walls and over the floor. One livid tongue of energy just flicked the detective's shin in passing.

It was like the impact of a sledgehammer. There was an instant of blindness and numb agony, and Harrison found himself sprawling, half-stunned on the floor. The lantern lay extinguished beside the overturned table, but the room was filled with a lurid light.

He realized that a bolt of lightning had struck the house, and that the upper story was ablaze. He hauled himself to his feet, looking for his gun. It lay halfway across the room, and as he started toward it, the bullet-split door swung open. Harrison stopped dead in his tracks.

Through the door limped a man naked but for a loin-cloth and moccasins on his feet. A revolver in his hand menaced the detective. Blood oozing from a wound in his thigh mingled with the paint with which he'd smeared on himself.

"So it was you who wanted to be the oil millionaire, Richard!" Harrison said.

Richard laughed savagely. "Aye, and I will be! And no cursed brothers to share with—brothers I always hated, damn them! Don't move! You nearly got me when you shot through the door. I'm taking no chances with you! But before I send you to Hell I'll tell you everything, as you deserve to know why you're about to die.

"As soon as you and Peter started for the graveyard, I realized my mistake in merely scratching the top of the grave—knew you'd hit hard clay and would know the grave hadn't been opened. I knew then I'd have to kill you, as well as Peter. I took the rat you mashed with your foot when neither of you were looking, so its disappearance would play on Peter's superstitions. I rode to the graveyard through the woods on a fast horse. The Indian disguise was one I thought up long ago.

"What with that rotten road and the flat that delayed you, I reached the graveyard before you and Peter did. On the way, though, I dismounted and stopped to kill that old fool Josh Sullivan. I was afraid he might recognize me if he saw me.

"I was watching when you dug into the grave. When Peter got panicky and ran through the woods I chased him, killed him, and brought his body here to the old house. Then I went back after you. I intended bringing your body here, or rather your bones, after the rats finished you, as I thought they would. Then I heard Joel Middleton coming and had to run for it. I don't care to meet that gun-fighting devil anywhere!

"I was going to burn this house with both your bodies in it. People would think when they found the bones in the ashes that Middleton killed you both and burned down the house to destroy the evidence! But despite the plan going awry, you still played right into my hands by coming here! Lightning has struck the house and it's burning! Oh, the gods are on my side tonight!"

A light of unholy madness played in Richard's eyes, but the pistol muzzle was steady. Harrison stood up, clenching his large fists helplessly.

"You'll lie here with that fool Peter!" Richard raved. "With a bullet through your head, until your bones are burned to such a crisp that no one can tell how you died! Joel Middleton will be shot down by some posse without a chance to talk. Saul will rave out his days in a madhouse! And I, who will be safely sleeping in my house in town before sun-up, will live out my allotted years in wealth and honor, never suspected, never..." He was sighting along the black barrel of his gun, eyes blazing, teeth bared like the fangs of a wolf between painted lips, his finger beginning to squeeze the trigger.

Harrison crouched tensely, desperately, poising to hurl himself with bare hands at the killer and try to pit his naked strength against the hot lead about to spit from that black muzzle.

Suddenly the door crashed inward behind Richard and the lurid glare framed a tall figure in a dripping slicker. An incoherent yell rang to the ceiling and the gun in Middleton's hand roared. Again and again, and yet again it fired, filling the room with smoke and thunder, and Richard's painted form jerked to the impact of the tearing lead bullets.

Through the smoke Harrison saw Richard Wilkinson toppling over, but he too was firing as he fell. Flames burst through the ceiling, and by their brighter glare Harrison saw him writhing on the floor, while a taller figure wavered in the doorway. Richard was screaming in agony.

Middleton threw his empty gun at Harrison's feet.

"Heard the shootin' and come to see," he croaked. "Reckon that settles the feud for good!" He toppled over and Harrison caught him in his arms, the man a lifeless weight.

Richard's screams rose to an unbearable pitch. The rats were swarming from their holes. Blood streaming across the floor had dripped into their holes, maddening them. Now they burst forth in a ravening horde that heeded not cries, or movement, or the devouring flames, but only their own fiendish hunger.

In a gray-black wave they swept over the dead man and the dying man. Peter's white face vanished under that wave. Richard's screaming grew thick and muffled. He writhed, half covered by gray, tearing figures who sucked at his gushing blood and tore at his flesh.

Harrison retreated through the door, carrying the dead outlaw. Joel Middleton may have been an outlaw and a killer, but he deserved a better fate than what was befalling his slayer.

Harrison wouldn't have lifted a finger to save Richard, even had it been in his power, which it wasn't. The graveyard rats had claimed their own.

Out in the yard, Harrison let his burden drop limply to the ground. Above the roar of the flames still rose those awful, smothered cries. Through the blazing doorway Harrison had a glimpse of a horror, a gory figure rearing upright, swaying, enveloped by a hundred clinging, tearing shapes. He glimpsed a face that wasn't a face at all, but a blind, bloody skull-mask. Then the awful scene was blotted out as the flaming roof fell with a thundering, ear-rending crash.

Sparks showered against the sky, the flames rose as the walls fell in, and Harrison staggered away, dragging the dead man with him, as a storm-wrapped dawn came haggardly over the oak-clad ridges.

KILLER PIPER

MEAGAN JEFFREY

Ben was the man to call when you had a rat problem. He was the only one who would come any time day or night to get them. He loved his job and loved rats. Ben didn't kill the rats he removed, though; instead he would catch them, cage them, then take them back home to his farm outside of town.

Ben lived in a town called Ghost Lake. The town was built around a glacier-fed, man-made lake located approximately forty-five kilometers west of the city of Calgary, Alberta. It was formed in 1929 with the completion of the Ghost Dam, and was developed on land leased from the Morley Indians by Calgary Power Ltd. It was an old and spooky town of over six thousand people. Most of the people there would drive to Calgary for work and shopping; it was mostly families of generations who lived in Ghost Lake.

The town had a very haunting tale to it. Only those who had lived there all of their lives knew if the tales were true, but they wouldn't speak about them. One of the most haunting stories was about children back in the 1940s who had gone missing and were never found. There were nineteen children from 1942-1946 who went missing without a trace. Some said it was the Lake monster, but others believed it was an old man they liked to call the 'Pied Piper.'

They said he would steal the children from their homes in the night, take them to his farm, and feed them to his rats, who would devour them skin and bone, leaving no trace of them to be found. No one was ever able to prove this, so the man was never held accountable for the missing children. But when the nineteenth child went missing, the townspeople decided that they'd had enough and went to the man's farm, burned down his barn where he kept all his pet rats, then hanged him in a tree outside of his house. It was said that his ghost still haunted the farm, but no one dared go up there. Except Ben, who bought the old farm, fixed it up, rebuilt the barn and now lives there.

No one speaks of the story any more, it's almost forgotten really. Most people just think that Ben's farm is haunted but don't really know by who or why. They've just passed the story along from generation to generation and it's been changed along the way.

Ben was a friendly young man, twenty-six years old. He had well-groomed dark hair, brown eyes, was about six feet tall, slender built, and always dressed in jeans and nice shirts or sweaters. Everyone loved him from the moment he moved to Ghost Lake about five years previous from Calgary. He moved to Ghost Lake because his rat catching business wasn't going so well in Calgary with all the other, bigger companies who were willing to kill the rats. Ben was kinder and more humane to them, and refused to kill them. Sort of like the old man.

So, Ben took his business to Ghost Lake, where he had read online that the town having a bad rat infestation problem. The townspeople were very grateful that he moved there to take the rats out of the town. They didn't know that he was keeping them up at his farm—alive.

Some of the older folks in town had started to talk about how Ben had mysteriously moved to Ghost Lake with a rat catching business and how it was too familiar to the old man who had killed the children. But they didn't speak outside one another, as to not to frighten the other people in town or cause Ben any problems…in case they were wrong.

Ben was out in his barn one nice spring day feeding the rats when his cell phone rang. When he answered, it was a young mother panicking over rats in her house. She was terrified they were going to attack her young infant son and asked Ben to come quickly to kill the rats. Ben hung up with the woman after getting her address and got in his red Dodge Ram 2500 and quickly drove to Ghost Lake.

When he arrived at the address, he saw the woman standing in her front yard with her baby in her arms. She ran up to Ben's truck when he parked it in the driveway, hysterical, saying that she refused to go back inside the house until the rats were gone. Ben told her to take her baby down to the local coffee shop and come back in about a half an hour. The woman agreed, got in her car, then drove away. Ben retrieved a cage and a bucket out of his truck and went inside the house. Once inside, he walked around slowly and quietly, listening for the rats. He went in the kitchen, placed the bucket on the table and the cage on the floor. He opened the lid to the bucket and took out a scoop of food, then set it inside the cage and sat in the chair. He began to whistle a soft, slow, very creepy song. After about a minute or two of whistling, the rats came around the corner into the kitchen from down the hall. At first he only saw two rats, then he saw four babies behind them. They walked right into the cage, started to nibble on the food, then sat down. Ben stood up, closed the cage and gently lifted it up onto the kitchen table. He closed the lid to the bucket and walked through the rest of the house.

He went into the living room, looked at the pictures and photographs hanging on the walls, sitting on tables and shelves. He lifted some to get a closer look and set them back down. Then he went down the hallway leading to the bedrooms. All the bedroom doors were open, so he peeked inside the first room. It was obviously the baby's room as it had pale blue walls, little teddy bears hanging with balloons and clouds, a fancy wooden crib and matching dresser, changing table and a rocking chair. He didn't bother to go into the baby's room. Instead, he walked to the next room, which was the mother's room. The walls were a dusty rose with a lighter shade of red carpet. There was a beautiful antique wood canopy bed, with gold curtains hanging around it and a red comforter and gold pillow cases. There was a matching antique wood dresser with a big mirror, vanity table and two end tables with some fancy lamps on each of them. He saw a beautiful old jewelry box sitting atop the dresser. He walked over and opened it. Inside were fancy gold and diamond rings, bracelets, necklaces and earrings. He touched a few, held up some, then put them all back. He didn't take anything. Next he went to the closet and opened it. He looked inside at all the clothes hanging neatly, then saw an old hat box sitting all alone on the top shelf. He pulled it down, walked over to the bed, put it on top of the mattress and opened it. He saw inside letters tied together tightly with a red ribbon, photographs under the letters and a ring box. He didn't untie the letters, but he did read who they were addressed to. The top one said it had been sent to a Mr. Dorling. Ben flipped the letters gently and saw they all had the same name to them. He put the letters on the bed next to the hat box and looked at the photographs. They were very old, black and white photos of a young man and woman. In some they were standing side by side, in others they were holding hands or kissing. On the back they all said Mary and Jonathan Dorling. Ben placed the photographs on top of the letters and picked up the ring box; he opened it. Inside it was a pair of gold wedding bands. He placed everything back in the hat box just as it was and returned it to the closet.

He left the room and went back to the kitchen, gathered his cage with rats and bucket, then headed to his truck. He set the cage and bucket in the back seat of the vehicle and stood next to it, waiting for the young mother to come back.

Not long after, the woman returned. She parked her car next to Ben's truck and before taking her baby out of the car, she asked Ben if he had caught the rats. He told her that there had been a family of rats, that he'd caught them all and she wouldn't have a rat problem anymore. The woman was very pleased, handed Ben seventy-five dollars and thanked him.

Ben thanked the woman for the money and work, wished her well, then headed back home. When he arrived, Ben took the cage to the barn and let the rats out into the giant cage he had built for them inside the barn. The barn had two feet deep concrete floors and twelve inch thick walls, so the rats couldn't dig down or out. He had a steel door just behind the wooden doors of the barn, so the rats couldn't chew through that. Once he let the new rats go inside the giant cage, he went inside with them and sat on the floor, closing the door behind him. The rats came right up and ate out of his hands as he smiled and petted them. He cared very much for these rodents and took good care of them.

"Now, guys, be nice to your new roommates. You'll all get out of here soon, like I promised," Ben said to the rats. The rats all looked at him, listening intently; they understood him. They all nodded in agreement.

Ben stood up and left the barn, closing the steel door tightly behind him and locking it. He went to his farm house, and after taking off his boots once inside and hanging up his coat, he went in the kitchen to wash his hands, make coffee, before going into the living room. He sat on his black leather arm chair. Placing his coffee on the table next to the chair, he picked up a notebook and pen off the table. He opened the book to a list of names and added 'Susan.' He looked at the names in the book with anger in his eyes. There were nineteen names on the list. He closed the book and held it tight in his hand, squeezing it hard, then put it back on the table with the pen next to it. He took a sip of his hot coffee then looked at the elderly man sitting on the black leather sofa across from him.

"When are you going to get started, Ben? What the hell are you waiting for?" the old man grumbled at him in a raspy voice. "You promised to do this for me."

Ben sighed and took another sip of his coffee before answering, "I just got the last one tonight. We'll start tomorrow night. I promise. I had to get the last one, you know that. Now relax, it'll happen," Ben snapped. Frustrated, he stood up, took his coffee and went into the kitchen again. He sipped from the cup one more time and then poured the rest down the sink. He went back in the living room, having to go through the room to get to the stairs to his bedroom. He saw that the old man was already gone. "Good." Ben grumbled to himself as he thumped up the stairs.

In his bedroom, he changed into some boxers and a t-shirt and went into the bathroom, washed up, and went to bed.

The next morning Ben awoke around eleven. Sitting up, he stretched. Before he could put his feet on the floor he saw the old man standing in the bedroom doorway looking at him. "What do you want now? I just woke up," Ben snarled at the old man.

"You start tonight. You have to do this, it's your destiny," the old man said. Ben closed his eyes, and when he opened them again, the old man was gone.

Ben shook his head, and sighed. He got out of bed and went into the bathroom to shower, then he dressed and went out to the barn. He went inside again and sat with the rats. "Tonight is the big night for some of you," he said. "I'll be taking fifteen of you with me tonight, so be ready. We'll leave once its dark and the people of Ghost Lake are sound asleep." Then stood up and walked out of the barn, locking the doors behind him again.

* * *

It was almost midnight before Ben had returned to the barn for his fifteen rats as he'd promised. He held open a big cage and fifteen rats ran inside it without him saying a word. He then took the rats with the notebook from the house in hand and closed and locked the barn doors. After loading the rats into the back seat of his truck, he drove into town. Ben parked on the corner of a nice street lined with old, fancy two and three-story homes. He opened the notebook and looked at the first name on the list, it was 'Tammy.' Ben closed the notebook, placed it on the seat next to him, then leaned back so he could see the rats in the cage

"Now, all of you remember what to do," Ben told the rats. They all were looking at him and they nodded, yes. "Okay, no screwing up, guys. We have to get through this list," Ben warned them. He climbed out of the truck and quietly closed his door and opened the back door of the vehicle, then he took the cage out and closed the door without a sound. He walked over to a house with a white picket fence and a red front door with the numbers 2314 on it.

Looking down at the rats in the cage, he nodded at them, put the cage down and silently opened its door. The rats ran out of the cage and right to the house, then around to the kitchen window that was left open just enough so that they could climb in easily.

Once inside, the rats ran to the front door, made a ladder out of themselves, and the top two rats unlocked the door for Ben. He silently walked inside and left the door open just a crack. He pointed to the upper floor and the rats ran up with Ben not far behind them. They went into the bedroom at the end of the hall as Ben went into the first room. He saw a baby sleeping soundly in its crib; he tiptoed over to the crib and snatched the baby, then ran out of the house to his truck. He went to the passenger side of the truck and put the baby in a car seat he had in the back. Quietly closing the door, he then ran back around to the driver's side, climbed in, and drove away without his lights on. He headed back to his farm, and left the rats at the house.

The rats crept into the parents' room and climbed onto the bed. The rats surrounded the sleeping parents and started to bite their necks hard, deep and fast, blood spraying across the bed sheets, comforter, walls, floor and the rats themselves. They were biting so hard and fast the man and woman didn't stand a chance at defending themselves or fleeing. They tried to scream, but their throats were already sliced open too deeply, so all they managed were gurgling sounds and gasps for whatever breaths they could before choking on their own blood. Once they were dead, the rats ran over to the dresser, stole whatever jewelry they could find, found the parents' wallets, and took those as well. Then they scurried out of the house and back to the farm where Ben was already waiting for them.

He was standing outside the barn waiting for the rats to return. When they did, they ran up to him and spit out the jewelry and wallets at his feet, then ran over to the barn door and sat and waited for him to open it. He gathered the items they'd brought him and opened the door for them. The rats quickly ran back inside and waited again.

Ben didn't close the door this time. Instead, he went over to the passenger side of the truck, took out the baby, and walked over to the barn. Before he went inside, he looked behind him at the old man standing at the doorway of his farm house, watching him. Ben turned back around and went inside the barn where the rats were all sitting on their hind legs, waiting for him.

He didn't look at the crying baby once. He took the baby, placed it on the floor, and quickly left the barn, closing and locking the door behind him. He ran back to the farm house, so he wouldn't have to hear the painful cries of the baby being devoured alive by the hundreds of rats in the barn. He slammed the front door behind him, ran upstairs to his bedroom, slammed that door, too, and turned on the TV, raising the volume as high as it would go. Sitting on the edge of his bed, he hunched over with his head in his hands.

"I can't believe you just made me do that, you bastard!" Ben yelled at the old man, who was now standing in his room with him.

"Don't you talk back to me, young man. You know why you have to do this. If you don't finish the list, you'll be just like them...*dead!* Do you understand me?" the old man snapped in reply.

Ben didn't look at the old man, he just sighed and said, "Yes, sir."

When Ben looked up again the old man was gone.

Ben turned his TV down and stood at his bedroom window; he heard nothing, just silence. He walked back over to his bed, took some sleeping pills from the night stand, then crawled under his blankets and fell asleep.

The next day, the mailman noticed that the front door to the house that Ben had been to the night before was open, which was unusual for this family, so he knocked, wanting to make sure everything was okay. When no one answered, he entered the home. He smelled the odor of blood and followed it to the parents' bedroom, shocked when he saw them sprawled out in the blood-soaked bed. He ran out of the room, down the stairs and out to the street, yelling for someone to help him. A neighbor heard his calls, and came out to see what all the noise was about. The man quickly explained what he saw and they called 9-1-1. Five minutes later, police and an ambulance arrived. Soon, the dead bodies were carried on stretchers and taken to the morgue. It wasn't long before TV news crews were there. They interviewed the mailman, took pictures of the house and talked to the police. By that afternoon, everyone in the town knew about the tragedy and were frightened.

That night the town was quiet, eerie and shut down early. People were afraid and the older people of the town were now whispering about the missing children and the killer from the 1940s.

Ben drove into the town that night with twenty rats this time. He set them free in another house. The same routine as before, but this time they had to go in through a dog door in the back of the house, run through the house to the front, where they then let him in. Ben was dressed in all black and was very careful not to be seen. He parked even further away this time. He had seen the news so he knew the people of the town were aware of what happened.

Again he went into the child's room and snatched a two-year-old girl. Covering her mouth so she couldn't scream, he ran out of the house and down the street to his truck. He took her back to his farm; just like the night before with the baby, and just like the night before, the rats were left to kill the parents. This time they didn't just kill them by biting their necks, though, this time they devoured their entire faces to the bone! They again took wallets and jewelry and went back to the farm to a waiting Ben.

"What the hell took you so long?" Ben demanded when the rats finally arrived. The rats just looked up at him and spit the wallets and jewelry onto the ground, then ran to the barn door that was already open for them. Ben went over to his truck, took out the crying toddler, carried her inside the barn, then left, locking her inside.

He sprinted into the house, to his bedroom, and cranked the volume of the TV high, then he sat on his bed with his head in hands.

The old man was standing in front of Ben, laughing at him. Angry, Ben stood up and yelled at him. *"What the fuck is so funny? How do you find any humor in this? You bastard."*

The old man wasn't laughing anymore; he glared at Ben, and said in such a tone that it shook Ben to his soul, "If you ever talk to me like that again, I won't hesitate to kill you." Then the old man vanished in front of Ben's eyes. The next thing Ben knew, the dresser in the corner of the room was flying across the bedroom at him, to crash against the wall with a loud bang.

"Okay! Okay! I'm sorry, Grandfather! I won't do it again. I'm sorry!" Ben cried out.

The next day the bodies were found at the second house and another statement was made on the news. Now the town was in a panic. They were worried about the two missing children from both homes and sad and scared about the parents of the children who'd been brutally attacked. They still didn't know it was rat attacks yet though, as the police hadn't given that information out.

Now the older people of the town weren't just whispering about how this was too much like the killings in the 1940s, they were openly speaking about it to everyone and anyone who would listen. People were terrified and making sure all their doors, windows and doors were locked.

That night before Ben went back to town for the third name on the list, his grandfather told him he would need to be extra careful, and that he would need to take the glass cutter with him to let the rats in the homes.

This time the old man wanted Ben to go to the rest of the homes on the list all in one night. Ben was worried he wouldn't be able to go to seventeen homes in one night without getting caught, but his grandfather told him how to do it and said it could be done.

Ben opened the barn door and whistled that eerie, slow song. Four hundred and fifty rats came out of the barn, all calm and all ready to follow Ben. This time the rats all squeezed in the back of the truck, and some went in the back seat and sat in the front with Ben.

He drove to the outside of Ghost Lake and let the rats out. Then house by house on the list, Ben went to one of the windows on the first floor and cut a small hole big enough for the rats to get in. One by one they entered, to then let Ben in and kill the parents after he took the small children. By the time Ben reached the seventeenth house he was exhausted, but again he cut a hole in the window, let the rats in and took the baby there. He ran back to his truck with the last child of the night and loaded it in with the other sixteen children who were scared and crying for their parents. Ben panicked, knowing all the crying was sure to attract attention and knew it was luck that no one had heard the children so far. He drove back to his farm and quickly unloaded all the children into the barn.

When he had the last of them inside, the rats were already back and running inside the barn to feed. Ben closed and locked the doors as before, but this time he got back in his truck and drove as far away from the farm as he could so he wouldn't hear all the screams and cries of the babies and toddlers being eaten alive by the hundreds of rats.

His grandfather watched him drive away; the old man wasn't pleased. But he let Ben go…for now.

The next day there was mass panic all across Ghost Lake. But when the seventeen families that were attacked were found, the townspeople weren't just terrified anymore, they were also *angry*!

The older people of the town who still remembered the deaths and missing children from the 1940s demanded the townspeople meet at the town hall to listen to what they had to say about the killings and missing children.

The entire town gathered in the hall and the six eldest people of the town told everyone about the man who had taken children in the night while they were sleeping back in the 1940s, took them to his farm—the same farm Ben lived at—and fed them to his rats.

They said how it was funny the way Ben came and took away the rats in the town but no one had ever seen him leave with any of the rats' bodies.

They said it was funny how Ben lived at the same farm as the man who killed the nineteen children years ago, and that again there were nineteen children missing.

How a man who apparently didn't know anything about Ghost Lake had suddenly moved to Ghost Lake from Calgary and bought up the farm that no one would or had lived in since the murderers of the missing kids of the 1940s.

The townspeople were shocked and furious. They wanted revenge, but they knew they needed proof.

That was when a young police woman came running into the hall and stood up in front of everyone, waving papers she held in her hands and yelling in anger and fear, "Listen to me! Ben isn't some stranger from out of town who by chance bought the farm and happened to be a rat exterminator. Ben is the great grandson of Jonathan Dorling! I found all the information in the police database when I did a background check on him! He's taking his grandfather's revenge out on the town and killing all those who killed his grandfather in the forties!"

The townspeople were silent and stunned. They couldn't believe what was happening to the town again.

They formed a plan, out of rage, to do what the townspeople did back in the 1940s and kill Ben like they killed his grandfather, only this time more brutally!

* * *

Ben returned to the farm when he was sure enough time had passed that he wouldn't hear any more screams or cries from the children. He parked his truck up close to his house and slowly walked inside, where his very unhappy grandfather was waiting for him.

"You ungrateful shit! Why did you leave?" his grandfather demanded to know.

Ben looked at him and said sadly, "I can't listen to the cries of the children. I'm not a monster like you."

Furious, his grandfather vanished again and started to throw around everything in the house. Chairs, dishes, cups, pictures, everything not nailed down was flying across the house, smashing into walls, and hitting Ben. He ducked down in the corner of the living room to hide and that was when he heard something outside the house. He ran to the front door and saw the headlights of cars pulling into his driveway through the small window on the door.

His grandfather appeared next to him, laughing loudly. "They're here to kill you; just like they killed me," the old man said in an evil laugh so loud it was deafening.

Ben covered his ears with his hands and yelled, "No, shut the hell up! Leave me alone! Get out of my head!"

His grandfather stopped laughing and vanished again. Ben watched as the mob of townspeople got out of their cars and trucks and surrounded the house. They were yelling, "Killer!" and "Murderer!" and that they were going to burn him alive in his house, slaughter him, beat him to death and hang him like his killer grandfather.

Ben was terrified. He sat on the floor with his back against the front door and waited for them to come for him. He knew there was nothing else he could do. Then he started to whistle that eerie, slow song loudly, calling the rats to him. The rodents heard the song and started to franticly claw against the concrete floor and walls of the barn. Because over four hundred rats were digging and biting at the same spot, the floor eventually began to chip and crack, and once the facade was removed, they digging became easier. Soon, there was a hole in the wall just large enough that they could get out one at a time.

The rats quickly scrambled out of the barn and went for the crowd of townspeople. A few of the people on the outside of the crowd saw the rats coming and started screaming; the people on the inside of the crowd were already pouring gas around Ben's house, ready to set fire to it.

Ben stood up and looked out the front door and saw people screaming and running from the rats. Then he saw one woman standing there watching him, watching the rats. She had a lighter in her hand; she walked up to the house where the gas was poured and set it on fire. She didn't run, she didn't scream, she just stood there and watched the fire spread around the house, burning the outside slowly, the flames getting higher and higher. Ben didn't back away from the door, he couldn't move. He was in a trance watching this woman.

The windows of the house cracked and shattered from the heat as the fire seeped into the house, burning everything, getting closer to Ben with each second. He started to cough from the smoke, and his eyes watered. He looked away to rub his eyes and cover his mouth. When he looked back out the window, the woman was gone.

His grandfather appeared next to him, smiling. "I knew this would come, that they would come and kill you. I needed you to finish what I started and to play out my revenge. You did your job and now, you can forever pay for your sins in hell with me," he said in a cold, evil, emotionless voice.

Ben looked at his grandfather and smiled. "I knew your plan all along, Grandfather, that's why I changed your list. The names on your list weren't the families of those who killed you long ago. Oh, no. They were the families of *your own blood line!*" Ben began laughing hysterically. His grandfather looked at him with shock and pain.

He screamed so loud it shook the walls of the burning house and all the people outside froze in place. Then the old man vanished, leaving Ben to burn in the house alone. Ben whistled his eerie, slow song, calling all the rats to come into the burning house with him. They ran inside as fast as they could, the people of the town watching them in confusion, horror, shock and happiness that the rodents were leaving them alone.

Once the last rat was inside with him, Ben looked out the window one last time and smiled at the people. He was ending the circle of terror once and for all, repaying them for the pain and heartache his grandfather had caused.

The door burst into flames, and the people could see flames all around and behind Ben, as the house began to crack and crumble. Ben screamed in pain as he was burned alive. The people heard his screams and the screeching of the rats until the house was completely engulfed in flames. Then they cheered and slowly left the farm, left it all to burn. It was finally over.

Later, the people of the town tore down everything at the farm. Taking away all memories and trace of what had happened there. Time passed and they moved on from the horror and pain of what Ben and his grandfather had done to them. They rebuilt and started to live happy and normal lives again.

But they didn't get everything at the farm. Ben had built an underground cellar to the barn, where he had the body of his grandfather, so the old man's soul could never rest.

The old man would always come back and do the same things again; always returning to kill off the townspeople. The old man's ghost was furious that his farm and everything on it was gone; he wanted revenge now like never before.

Slowly he began calling the rats in the surrounding woods to him, and with each day, the rodents appeared, all congregating on the bare patch of earth where the cellar was buried.

And when he had enough, he would release them on the town, and this time he wouldn't fail. Thousands of rats would attack, kill and devour the townspeople alive; every one of them. Every person: young and old, toddler or teen. The rats would get every last one.

Then, when the town was utterly destroyed, he would wait for the next group of people to come and start all over again.

THE RATS IN THE WALLS

H.P. LOVECRAFT

On 16 July 1923, I moved into Exham Priory after the last workman had finished his labors. The restoration had been a stupendous task, for little had remained of the deserted pile but a shell-like ruin, yet because it had been the seat of my ancestors, I let no expense deter me.

The place had not been inhabited since the reign of James the First, when a tragedy of intensely hideous, though largely unexplained nature, had struck down the master, five of his children, and several servants, and driven forth under a cloud of suspicion and terror the third son, my lineal progenitor, and the only survivor of the abhorred line.

With this sole heir denounced as a murderer, the estate had reverted to the crown, nor had the accused man made any attempt to exculpate himself or regain his property. Shaken by some horror greater than that of conscience or the law — and expressing only a frantic wish to exclude the ancient edifice from his sight and memory—Walter de la Poer, eleventh Baron Exham, fled to Virginia and there founded the family which by the next century had become known as Delapore.

Exham Priory had remained untenanted, though later allotted to the estates of the Norrys family and much studied because of its peculiarly composite architecture; an architecture involving Gothic towers resting on a Saxon or Romanesque substructure, whose foundation in turn was of a still earlier order or blend of orders-Roman, and even Druidic or native Cymric, if legends speak truly. This foundation was a very singular thing, being merged on one side with the solid limestone of the precipice from whose brink the priory overlooked a desolate valley three miles west of the village of Anchester.

Architects and antiquarians loved to examine this strange relic of forgotten centuries, but the country folk hated it. They had hated it hundreds of years before, when my ancestors lived there, and they hated it now, with the moss and mold of abandonment on it.

I had not been a day in Anchester before I knew I came of an accursed house, and this week workmen have blown up Exham Priory, and are busy obliterating the traces of its foundations. The bare statistics of my ancestry I had always known, together with the fact that my first American forebear had come to the colonies under a strange cloud. Of details, however, I had been kept fully ignorant through the policy of reticence always maintained by the Delapores.

Unlike our planter neighbors, we seldom boasted of crusading ancestors or other medieval and Renaissance heroes, nor was any kind of tradition handed down except what may have been recorded in the sealed envelope left before the Civil War by every squire to his eldest son for posthumous opening. The glories we cherished were those achieved since the migration. The glories of a proud and honorable, if somewhat reserved and unsocial Virginia line.

During the war, our fortunes were extinguished and our entire existence changed by the burning of Carfax, our home on the banks of the James. My grandfather, advanced in years, had perished in that incendiary outrage, and with him the envelope that had bound us all to the past. I can recall that fire today as I saw it then at the age of seven, with the federal soldiers shouting, the women screaming, and the blacks howling and praying. My father was in the army, defending Richmond, and after many formalities my mother and I were passed through the lines to join him.

When the war ended we all moved north, whence my mother had come, and I grew to manhood, middle age, and ultimate wealth as a stolid Yankee. Neither my father nor I ever knew what our hereditary envelope had contained, and as I merged into the grayness of Massachusetts business life, I lost all interest in the mysteries which evidently lurked far back in my family tree. Had I suspected their nature, how gladly I would have left Exham Priory to its moss, bats and cobwebs!

My father died in 1904, but without any message to leave to me, or to my only child, Alfred, a motherless boy of ten. It was this boy who reversed the order of family information, for although I could give him only jesting conjectures about the past, he wrote me of some very interesting ancestral legends when the late war took him to England in 1917 as an aviation officer.

Apparently the Delapores had a colorful and perhaps sinister history, for a friend of my son's, Capt. Edward Norrys of the Royal Flying Corps, lived near the family seat at Anchester and related some peasant superstitions which few novelists could equal for wildness and incredibility. Norrys himself, of course, did not take them so seriously; but they amused my son and made good material for his letters to me. It was this legendry which definitely turned my attention to my transatlantic heritage, and made me resolve to purchase and restore the family seat which Norrys showed to Alfred in its picturesque desertion, and offered to get for him at a surprisingly reasonable figure, since his own uncle was the present owner.

I bought Exham Priory in 1918, but was almost immediately distracted from my plans of restoration by the return of my son as a maimed invalid.

During the two years that he lived, I thought of nothing but his care, having even placed my business under the direction of partners.

In 1921, as I found myself bereaved and aimless, and a retired manufacturer no longer young, I resolved to divert my remaining years with my new possession. Visiting Anchester in December, I was entertained by Capt. Norrys, a plump, amiable young man who had thought much of my son, and I secured his assistance in gathering plans and anecdotes to guide in the coming restoration.

I saw Exham Priory itself without emotion; a jumble of tottering medieval ruins covered with lichens and honeycombed with rooks' nests, perched perilously upon a precipice, and denuded of floors or other interior features save the stone walls of the separate towers.

As I gradually recovered the image of the edifice as it had been when my ancestors left it over three centuries before, I began to hire workmen for the reconstruction. In every case I was forced to go outside the immediate locality, for the Anchester villagers had an almost unbelievable fear and hatred of the place. The sentiment was so great that it was sometimes communicated to the outside laborers, causing numerous desertions, while its scope appeared to include both the priory and its ancient family.

My son had told me that he was somewhat avoided during his visits because he was a de la Poer, and I now found myself subtly ostracized for a like reason until I convinced the peasants how little I knew of my heritage.

Even then they sullenly disliked me, so that I had to collect most of the village traditions through the mediation of Norrys. What the people could not forgive, perhaps, was that I had come to restore a symbol so abhorrent to them, for rationally or not, they viewed Exham Priory as nothing less than a haunt of fiends and werewolves.

Piecing together the tales which Norrys collected for me, and supplementing them with the accounts of several savants who had studied the ruins, I deduced that Exham Priory stood on the site of a prehistoric temple, a Druidical or ante-Druidical thing which must have been contemporary with Stonehenge.

That indescribable rites had been celebrated there, few doubted, and there were unpleasant tales of the transference of these rites into the Cybele worship which the Romans had introduced.

Inscriptions still visible in the sub-cellar bore such unmistakable letters as **DIV...OPS...MAGNA. MAT**... A sign of the Magna Mater whose dark worship was once vainly forbidden to Roman citizens.

Anchester had been the camp of the third Augustan legion, as many remains attest, and it was said that the temple of Cybele was splendid and thronged with worshippers that performed nameless ceremonies at the bidding of a Phrygian priest. Tales added that the fall of the old religion did not end the orgies at the temple, but that the priests lived on in the new faith without real change.

Likewise was it said that the rites did not vanish with the Roman power, and that certain among the Saxons added to what remained of the temple, and gave it the essential outline it subsequently preserved, making it the center of a cult feared through half the *heptarchy*. About 1000 A.D. the place is mentioned in a chronicle as being a substantial stone priory housing a strange and powerful monastic order, and surrounded by extensive gardens which needed no walls to exclude a frightened populace.

It was never destroyed by the Danes, though after the Norman Conquest it must have declined tremendously, since there was no impediment when Henry the Third granted the site to my ancestor, Gilbert de la Poer, First Baron Exham, in 1261.

Of my family before this date there is no evil report, but something strange must have happened then. In one chronicle there is a reference to a de la Poer as 'cursed of God in 1307,' while village legendry had nothing but evil and frantic fear to tell of the castle that went up on the foundations of the old temple and priory.

The fireside tales were of the most grisly description, all the ghastlier because of their frightened reticence and cloudy evasiveness. They represented my ancestors as a race of hereditary demons beside whom Gilles de Retz and the Marquis de Sade would seem tame, and hinted whisperingly at their responsibility for the occasional disappearances of villagers through several generations.

The worst characters, apparently, were the barons and their direct heirs; at least, most was whispered about these. If of healthier inclinations, it was said, an heir would early and mysteriously die to make way for another more typical scion. There seemed to be an inner cult in the family, presided over by the head of the house, and sometimes closed except to a few members.

Temperament rather than ancestry was evidently the basis of this cult, for it was entered by several who married into the family. Lady Margaret Trevor from Cornwall, wife of Godfrey, the second son of the fifth baron, became a favorite bane of children all over the countryside, and the demon heroine of a particularly horrible old ballad not yet extinct near the Welsh border. Preserved in balladry, too, though not illustrating the same point, is the hideous tale of Lady Mary de la Poer, who shortly after her marriage to the Earl of Shrewsfield, was killed by him and his mother, both of the slayers being absolved and blessed by the priest to whom they confessed what they dared not repeat to the world.

These myths and ballads, typical as they were of crude superstition, repelled me greatly. Their persistence, and their application to so long a line of my ancestors, were especially annoying, while the imputations of monstrous habits proved unpleasantly reminiscent of the one known scandal of my immediate forebears—the case of my cousin, young Randolph Delapore of Carfax who went among the blacks and became a voodoo priest after he returned from the Mexican War.

I was much less disturbed by the vague tales of wails and howlings in the barren, windswept valley beneath the limestone cliff, and of the graveyard stenches after the spring rains, the floundering, squealing white thing on which Sir John Clave's horse had trod one night in a lonely field, and of the servant that had gone mad at what he saw in the priory in the full light of day.

These things were hackneyed, spectral lore, and I was at that time a pronounced skeptic. The accounts of vanished peasants were less to be dismissed, though not especially significant in view of medieval custom. Prying curiosity meant death, and more than one severed head had been publicly shown on the bastions—now effaced—around Exham Priory.

A few of the tales were exceedingly picturesque, and made me wish I had learned more of the comparative mythology in my youth. There was for instance, the belief that a legion of bat-winged devils kept Witches' Sabbath each night at the priory—a legion whose sustenance might explain the disproportionate abundance of coarse vegetables harvested in the vast gardens. But most vivid of all, there was the dramatic epic of the rats—the scampering army of obscene vermin which had burst forth from the castle three months after the tragedy that doomed it to desertion—the lean, filthy, ravenous army which had swept all before it and devoured fowl, cats, dogs, hogs, sheep, and even two hapless human beings before its fury was spent. Around that unforgettable rodent army a whole separate cycle of myths revolves, for it scattered among the village homes and brought curses and horrors in its wake.

Such was the lore that assailed me as I pushed to completion, with an elderly obstinacy, the work of restoring my ancestral home. It must not be imagined for a moment that these tales formed my principal psychological environment. On the other hand, I was constantly praised and encouraged by Capt. Norrys and the antiquarians who surrounded and aided me.

When the task was done, over two years after its commencement, I viewed the great rooms, wainscoted walls, vaulted ceilings, mullioned windows, and broad staircases with a pride which fully compensated for the prodigious expense of the restoration.

Every attribute of the Middle Ages was cunningly reproduced and the new parts blended perfectly with the original walls and foundations. The seat of my fathers was complete, and I looked forward to redeeming at last the local fame of the line which ended in me. I could reside here permanently, and prove that a de la Poer—for I had adopted again the original spelling of the name—need not be a fiend. My comfort was perhaps augmented by the fact that, although Exham Priory was medievally fitted, its interior was in truth wholly new and free from old vermin and old ghosts alike.

As I have said, I moved in on July 16, 1923. My household consisted of seven servants and nine cats, of which latter species I am particularly fond of. My eldest cat, 'Nigel,' was seven years old and had come with me from my home in Bolton, Massachusetts; the others I had accumulated while living with Capt. Norrys' family during the restoration of the priory.

For five days our routine proceeded with the utmost placidity, my time being spent mostly in the codification of old family data. I had now obtained some very circumstantial accounts of the final tragedy and flight of Walter de la Poer, which I conceived to be the probable contents of the hereditary paper lost in the fire at Carfax. It appeared that my ancestor was accused with much reason of having killed all the other members of his household, except four servant confederates, in their sleep, about two weeks after a shocking discovery which changed his entire demeanor, but which except by implication, he disclosed to no one save perhaps the servants who assisted him and afterwards fled beyond reach.

This deliberate slaughter—which included a father, three brothers, and two sisters—was largely condoned by the villagers, and was so slackly treated by the law that its perpetrator escaped honored, unharmed, and undisguised to Virginia. The general whispered sentiment was that he had purged the land of an immemorial curse. What discovery had prompted an act so terrible, I could scarcely even conjecture. Walter de la Poer must have known for years the sinister tales about his family, so that this material could have given him no fresh impulse. Had he then, witnessed some appalling ancient rite, or stumbled upon some frightful and revealing symbol in the priory or its vicinity?

He was reputed to have been a shy, gentle youth in England. In Virginia he seemed not so much hard or bitter as harassed and apprehensive. He was spoken of in the diary of another gentleman adventurer, Francis Harley of Bellview, as a man of unexampled justice, honor, and delicacy.

On July 22, occurred the first incident which, though lightly dismissed at the time, takes on a preternatural significance in relation to later events. It was so simple as to be almost negligible, and could not possibly have been noticed under the circumstances. It must be recalled that since I was in a building practically fresh and new except for the walls, and surrounded by a well-balanced staff of servitors, apprehension would have been absurd despite the locality.

What I afterward remembered is merely this—that my old black cat, whose moods I know so well, was undoubtedly alert and anxious to an extent wholly out of keeping with his natural character. He roved from room to room, restless and disturbed, and sniffed constantly about the walls which formed part of the Gothic structure. I realize how trite this sounds—like the inevitable dog in the ghost story, which always growls before his master sees the sheeted figure—yet I cannot consistently suppress it.

The following day a servant complained of restlessness among all the cats in the house. He came to me in my study, a lofty west room on the second story, with high arches, black oak paneling, and a triple Gothic window overlooking the limestone cliff and desolate valley. Even as he spoke, I saw the jetty form of Nigel creeping along the west wall, the cat scratching at the new panels that overlaid the ancient stone.

I told the servant that there must be a singular odor or emanation from the old stonework, imperceptible to humans, but affecting the delicate senses of cats even through the new woodwork. This I truly believed, and when the fellow suggested the presence of mice or rats, I mentioned that there had been no rats there for three hundred years, and that even the field mice of the surrounding country could hardly be found in these high walls, where the rodents had never been known to stray. That afternoon I called on Capt. Norrys, and he assured me that it would be quite incredible for field mice to infest the priory in such a sudden and unprecedented fashion.

That night, dispensing as usual with a valet, I retired in the west tower chamber which I had chosen as my own, the room reached from the study by a stone staircase and short gallery—the former partly ancient, the latter entirely restored. This room was circular, very high, and without wainscoting, being hung with tapestries which I had personally chosen in London.

Seeing that Nigel was with me, I closed the heavy Gothic door and retired by the light of the electric bulbs which so cleverly counterfeited candles, finally switching off the light and sinking on the carved and canopied four-poster bed, with the venerable cat in his accustomed place across my feet. I did not draw the curtains, but gazed out at the narrow window which I faced. There was a suspicion of aurora in the sky, and the delicate traceries of the window were pleasantly silhouetted.

At some time I must have fallen quietly asleep, for I recall a distinct sense of leaving strange dreams, when Nigel started violently from his placid position. I saw him in the faint auroral glow, head strained forward, fore feet on my ankles, and hind feet stretched behind. He was looking intensely at a point on the wall somewhat west of the window, a point which to my eye had nothing to mark it, but toward which all my attention was now directed.

And as I watched, I knew that Nigel was not vainly excited. Whether the tapestry hanging on the wall actually moved I cannot say. I think it did, very slightly. But what I can swear to is that behind it I heard a low, distinct scurrying as of rats or mice. In a moment the cat had jumped bodily on the screening tapestry, bringing the affected section to the floor with his weight, and exposing a damp, ancient wall of stone, patched here and there by the restorers, and devoid of any trace of rodent prowlers.

Nigel raced up and down the floor by this part of the wall, clawing the fallen tapestry and seemingly trying at times to insert a paw between the wall and the oaken floor. He found nothing, and after a time returned wearily to his place across my feet. I had not moved, but I did not sleep again that night.

In the morning I questioned all the servants, and found that none of them had noticed anything unusual, save that the cook remembered the actions of another cat which had rested on her windowsill. This cat had begun howling at some unknown hour of the night, awaking the cook in time for her to see him dart purposefully out of the open door and down the stairs.

I drowsed away the noontime, and in the afternoon called again on Capt. Norrys, who became exceedingly interested in what I told him. The odd incidents—so slight yet so curious—appealed to his sense of the picturesque and elicited from him a number of reminiscences of local ghostly lore. We were genuinely perplexed at the presence of rats, and Norrys lent me some traps and Paris green, which I had the servants place in strategic locations when I returned.

I retired early, being very sleepy, but was harassed by dreams of the most horrible sort. I seemed to be looking down from an immense height upon a grotto, knee-deep with filth, where a white-bearded demon swineherd drove about with his staff a flock of fungous, flabby beasts whose appearance filled me with unutterable loathing. Then, as the swineherd paused and nodded over his task, a mighty swarm of rats rained down on the stinking abyss and fell to devouring beasts and man alike.

From this terrific vision I was abruptly awakened by the motions of Nigel, who had been sleeping as usual across my feet. This time I did not have to question the source of his snarls and hisses, and of the fear which made him sink his claws into my ankle, unconscious of their effect, for on every side of the chamber the walls were alive with nauseous sound. It was the venomous slithering of ravenous, gigantic rats. There was now no aurora to show the state of the tapestry—the fallen section of which had been replaced—but I was not too frightened to switch on the light.

As the bulbs leapt into radiance, I saw a hideous shaking all over the tapestry, causing the somewhat peculiar designs to execute a singular dance of death. This motion disappeared almost at once, and the sound with it.

Springing out of bed, I poked at the tapestry with the long handle of a warming-pan that rested near, and lifted one section to see what lay beneath. There was nothing but the patched stone wall, and even the cat had lost his tense realization of abnormal presences. When I examined the circular trap that had been placed in the room, I found all of the openings sprung, though no trace remained of what had been caught and had escaped.

Further sleep was out of the question, so lighting a candle, I opened the door and went out in the gallery towards the stairs to my study, Nigel following at my heels. Before we had reached the stone steps, however, the cat darted ahead of me and vanished down the ancient steps. As I descended the stairs myself, I became suddenly aware of sounds in the great room below, sounds of a nature which could not be mistaken.

The oak-paneled walls were alive with rats, scampering and milling while Nigel was racing about with the fury of a baffled hunter. Reaching the bottom, I switched on the light, which did not this time cause the noise to subside. The rats continued their riot, stampeding with such force and distinctness that I could finally assign to their motions a definite direction. These creatures, in numbers apparently inexhaustible, were engaged in one stupendous migration from inconceivable heights to some depth conceivably or inconceivably below.

I then heard footsteps in the corridor, and in another moment two servants pushed open the massive door. They were searching the house for some unknown source of disturbance which had thrown all the cats into a snarling panic and caused them to plunge precipitately down several flights of stairs, and to squat yowling before the closed door to the sub-cellar. I asked them if they had heard the rats, but they replied in the negative, and when I turned to call their attention to the sounds in the wall panels, I realized that the noise had ceased.

With the two men, I went down to the door of the sub-cellar, but found the cats already dispersed. Later, I resolved to explore the crypt below, but for the present I merely made a round of the traps. All were sprung, yet all were empty. Satisfying myself that no one had heard the rats save the cats and me, I sat in my study till morning, thinking profoundly and recalling every scrap of legend I had unearthed concerning the building I inhabited. I slept some in the afternoon, leaning back in the one comfortable library chair which my medieval plan of furnishing could not banish. Later, I telephoned Capt. Norrys, who came over and helped me explore the sub-cellar.

Absolutely nothing untoward was found, although we could not repress a thrill at the knowledge that this vault was built by Roman hands. Every low arch and massive pillar was Roman—not the debased Romanesque of the bungling Saxons, but the severe and harmonious classicism of the age of the Caesars. Indeed, the walls abounded with inscriptions familiar to the antiquarians who had repeatedly explored the place. Things like 'P. GETAE. PROP...TEMP...DONA...' and 'L. PRAEG...VS...PONTIFI...ATYS.'

The reference to Atys made me shiver, for I had read Catullus and knew something of the hideous rites of the Eastern god, whose worship was so mixed with that of Cybele. Norrys and I, by the light of lanterns, tried to interpret the odd and nearly destroyed designs on certain irregular rectangular blocks of stone generally held to be altars, but we could make nothing of them. We remembered that one pattern, a sort of rayed sun, was held by students to imply a non-Roman origin, suggesting that the altars had merely been adopted by the Roman priests from some older and perhaps aboriginal temple on the same site. On one of the blocks were some brown stains which made me wonder. The largest, in the center of the room, had certain features on the upper surface which indicated its connection with fire—probably burnt offerings.

Such were the sights in the crypt that the cats had howled at the door, and where Norrys and I now determined to pass the night. Couches were brought down by the servants, who were told not to mind any nocturnal actions of the cats, and Nigel was admitted as much for help as for companionship. We decided to keep the great oak door—a modern replica with slits for ventilation—tightly closed, and with this attended to, we retired with lanterns still burning to wait for whatever might occur.

The vault was very deep in the foundations of the priory, and undoubtedly far down on the face of the beetling limestone cliff overlooking the waste valley.

That it had been the goal of the scuffling and unexplainable rats I could not doubt, though why I could not tell. As we lay there expectantly, I found my vigil occasionally mixed with half-formed dreams from which the uneasy motions of the cat across my feet would rouse me.

These dreams were not wholesome, but horrible, like the one I had the night before. I saw again the grotto, and the swineherd with his unmentionable fungous beasts wallowing in filth. As I looked at these things, they seemed nearer and more distinct—so distinct that I could almost observe their features.

Then I did observe the flabby features of one of them, and awakened with such a scream that Nigel jumped up, while Capt. Norrys, who had not slept, laughed considerably. Norrys might have laughed more—or perhaps less—had he known what it was that had made me scream. But I did not remember myself till later. Ultimate horror often paralyses memory in a merciful way.

Norrys waked me when the phenomena began. Out of the same frightful dream, I was called by his gentle shaking and his urging to listen to the cats. Indeed, there was much to listen to, for beyond the closed door at the head of the stone steps, was a veritable nightmare of feline yelling and clawing, while Nigel, unmindful of his kindred outside, was running excitedly round the bare stone walls, in which I heard the same sound of scurrying rats that had troubled me the night before.

An acute terror rose within me, for here were anomalies which nothing normal could explain. These rats, if not the creatures of a madness which I shared with the cats alone, must be burrowing and sliding in walls I had thought to be solid limestone blocks...unless perhaps the action of water through more than seventeen centuries had eaten winding tunnels which rodent bodies had worn clear and ample. But even so, the spectral horror was no less, for if these were living vermin, why did not Norrys hear their disgusting commotion? Why did he urge me to watch Nigel and listen to the cats outside, and why did he guess wildly and vaguely at what could have aroused them?

By the time I had managed to tell him, as rationally as I could, what I thought I was hearing, I heard the last fading impression of scurrying, which had retreated still downward, far underneath the deepest of sub-cellars till it seemed as if the entire cliff below were riddled with questing rats.

Norrys was not as skeptical as I had anticipated, but instead seemed profoundly moved. He motioned to me to notice that the cats at the door had ceased their clamor, as if giving up the rats for lost, while Nigel had a burst of renewed restlessness, and was clawing frantically around the bottom of the large stone altar in the center of the room, which was nearer Norrys' couch than mine.

My fear of the unknown was at this point very great. Something astounding had occurred, and I saw that Capt. Norrys, a younger, stouter, and presumably more naturally materialistic man, was affected fully as much as myself—perhaps because of his lifelong and intimate familiarity with local legend. We could for the moment do nothing but watch the old black cat as he pawed with decreasing fervor at the base of the altar, occasionally looking up and mewing to me in that persuasive manner which he used when he wished me to perform some favor for him.

Norrys took a lantern close to the altar and examined the place where Nigel was pawing, then silently knelt and scraped away the lichens of the centuries which joined the massive pre-Roman block to the mosaic-covered stone floor. He did not find anything, and was about to abandon his efforts when I noticed a trivial circumstance which made me shudder, even though it implied nothing more than I had already imagined.

I told him of it, and we both looked at its almost imperceptible manifestation with the fixedness of fascinated discovery and acknowledgment. It was that the flame of the lantern set down near the altar was slightly but certainly flickering from a draught of air which it had not before received, and which definitely came from the crevice between the floor and altar, where Norrys was scraping away the lichens.

We spent the rest of the night in my brilliantly-lighted study, nervously discussing what we should do next. The discovery that some vault deeper than the deepest known masonry of the Romans was under this accursed priory, some vault unsuspected by the curious antiquarians of the past three centuries, would have been sufficient to excite us, even without any background of the sinister.

As it was, the fascination became two-fold, and we paused, in doubt whether to abandon our search and quit the priory forever in superstitious caution, or to gratify our sense of adventure and brave whatever horrors might await us in the unknown depths.

By morning we had compromised, and decided to go to London to gather a group of archaeologists and scientific men fit to cope with the mystery. It should be mentioned that before leaving the sub-cellar we had vainly tried to move the central altar which we now recognized as the gate to a new pit of nameless fear. What secret would open the gate, wiser men than we would have to find.

During many days in London, Capt. Norrys and I presented our facts, conjectures, and legendary anecdotes to five eminent authorities, all men who could be trusted to respect any family disclosures which future explorations might develop.

We found most of them little disposed to scoff, but instead they were intensely interested and sincerely sympathetic. It is hardly necessary to name them all, but I may say that they included Sir William Brinton, whose excavations in the Troad excited most of the world in their day. As we all took the train back to Anchester, I felt myself poised on the brink of frightful revelations, a sensation symbolized by the air of mourning among the many Americans at the unexpected death of the President on the other side of the world.

On the evening of August 7, we reached Exham Priory, where the servants assured me that nothing unusual had occurred. The cats, even old Nigel, had been perfectly placid, and not a trap in the house had been sprung. We were to begin exploring on the following day, so I assigned well-appointed rooms to all my guests.

I retired in my own tower chamber, with Nigel across my feet. Sleep came quickly, but hideous dreams assailed me. There was a vision of a Roman feast like that of Trimalchio, with a horror in a covered platter. Then came that damnable, recurrent thing about the swineherd in the grotto.

When I awoke it was full daylight, with normal sounds in the house below. The rats, living or spectral, had not troubled me, and Nigel was still quietly asleep. On going down, I found that the same tranquility had prevailed elsewhere, a condition which one of the assembled servants—a fellow named Thornton, devoted to the psychic—rather absurdly laid to the fact that I had now been shown the thing which certain forces had wished to show me.

All was now ready, and at eleven in the morning, our entire group of seven men, bearing powerful electric searchlights and implements of excavation, went down to the sub-cellar and bolted the door behind us. Nigel was with us, for the investigators found no occasion to despise his excitability, and were indeed anxious that he be present in case of obscure rodent manifestations.

We noted the Roman inscriptions and unknown altar designs only briefly, for three of the scholars had already seen them, and all knew their characteristics. Prime attention was paid to the momentous central altar, and within an hour Sir William Brinton had caused it to tilt backward, balanced by some unknown counterweight.

Such a horror was revealed that it would have overwhelmed us had we not been prepared. Through a nearly square opening in the tiled floor, sprawling on a flight of stone steps so worn that it was little more than an inclined plane at the center, was a ghastly array of human or semi-human bones. Those which retained their shape as skeletons showed attitudes of panic and fear, and over all were the marks of rodent gnawings. The skulls denoted nothing short of utter idiocy, cretinism, or primitive semi-apedom.

Above the hellishly littered steps arched a descending passage, seemingly chiseled from the solid rock, and conducting a current of air.

This current was not a sudden and noxious rush as from a closed vault, but a cool breeze with something of freshness in it. We did not pause long, but began to clear a passage down the steps as we shivered. It was then that Sir William, examining the hewn walls, made the odd observation that the passage, according to the direction of the strokes, must have been chiseled from below.

After going down a few steps amidst the gnawed bones, we saw that there was light ahead; not any mystic phosphorescence, but a filtered daylight which could not come except from unknown fissures in the cliff that overlooked the waste valley.

That such fissures had escaped notice from outside was hardly remarkable, for not only is the valley completely uninhabited, but the cliff is so high that only an aeronaut could study its face in detail.

A few steps more and our breaths were literally snatched from us by what we saw; so literally that Thornton, the psychic investigator, actually fainted in the arms of the dazed men who stood behind him.

Norrys, his plump face utterly white and flabby, simply cried out inarticulately, while I think that what I did was to gasp or hiss, and cover my eyes.

The man behind me—the only one of the party older than I—croaked the hackneyed, "My God!" in the most cracked voice I have ever heard. Of seven cultivated men, only Sir William Brinton retained his composure, a thing the more to his credit because he led the party and must have seen the sight first.

It was a grotto of enormous height, stretching away farther than any eye could see—a subterranean world of limitless mystery and horrible suggestion.

There were buildings and other architectural remains—in one terrified glance I saw a weird pattern of tumuli, a savage circle of monoliths, a low-domed Roman ruin, a sprawling Saxon pile, and an early English edifice of wood—but all these were dwarfed by the ghoulish spectacle presented by the general surface of the ground.

Yards around the steps extended an insane tangle of human bones, or bones at least as human as those on the steps. Like a foamy sea they stretched, some fallen apart, but others wholly or partly articulated as skeletons. The latter were invariably in postures of demonic frenzy, either fighting off some menace or clutching other forms with cannibal intent.

When Dr. Trask, the anthropologist, stopped to classify the skulls, he found a degraded mixture which utterly baffled him. They were mostly lower than the Piltdown man in the scale of evolution, but in every case definitely human. Many were of higher grade, and a very few were the skulls of supremely and sensitively developed types. All the bones were gnawed, mostly by rats, but some by others of the half-human drove.

Mixed with them were many tiny bones of rats—fallen members of the lethal army which closed the ancient epic.

I wonder that any man among us lived and kept his sanity through that hideous day of discovery. Not Hoffman nor Huysmans could conceive a scene more wildly incredible, more frenetically repellent, or more Gothically grotesque than the gloom-filled grotto through which we seven staggered, each stumbling on revelation after revelation, and trying to keep for the nonce from thinking of the events which must have taken place there three hundred, a thousand, two thousand or perhaps ten thousand years ago.

It was the antechamber of hell, and poor Thornton fainted again when Trask told him that some of the skeleton things must have descended as quadrupeds through the last twenty or more generations.

Horror piled on horror as we began to interpret the architectural remains. The quadruped things—with their occasional recruits from the biped class—had been kept in stone pens, out of which they must have broken in their last delirium of hunger or fear of the rats.

There had been great herds of them, evidently fattened on the coarse vegetables whose remains could be found as a sort of poisonous ensilage at the bottom of the huge stone bins older than Rome. I knew now why my ancestors had had such excessive gardens—would to heaven I could forget! The purpose of the herds I did not have to ask.

Sir William, standing with his searchlight in the Roman ruin, translated aloud the most shocking ritual I have ever known, and told of the diet of the antediluvian cult which the priests of Cybele found and mingled with their own.

Norrys, used as he was to the trenches, could not walk straight when he came out of one of the buildings. It was a butcher shop and kitchen—he had expected that—but it was too much to see familiar English implements in such a place, and to read familiar English graffiti there, some as recent as 1610. I could not go in that building—that building whose demon activities were stopped only by the dagger of my ancestor Walter de la Poer.

What I did venture to enter was the low Saxon building whose oaken door had fallen, and there I found a terrible row of ten stone cells with rusty bars. Three had tenants, all skeletons of high grade, and on the bony forefinger of one I found a ring with my own coat-of-arms.

Sir William found a vault with far older cells below the Roman chapel, but these cells were empty. Below them was a low crypt with cases of formally arranged bones, some of them bearing terrible parallel inscriptions carved in Latin, Greek, and the tongue of Phyrgia.

Meanwhile, Dr. Trask had opened one of the prehistoric tumuli, and brought to light skulls which were slightly more human than a gorilla's, and which bore indescribably ideographic carvings.

Through all this horror my cat stalked unperturbed. Once I saw him monstrously perched atop a mountain of bones, and wondered at the secrets that might lie behind his yellow eyes.

Having grasped to some slight degree the frightful revelations of this area—an area so hideously foreshadowed by my recurrent dream—we turned to that apparently boundless depth of midnight cavern where no ray of light from the cliff could penetrate.

We shall never know what sightless Stygian worlds yawned beyond the little distance we went, for it was decided that such secrets were not good for mankind.

But there was plenty to engross us close at hand, for we had not gone far before the searchlights showed that accursed infinity of pits in which the rats had feasted, and whose sudden lack of replenishment had driven the ravenous rodent army first to turn on the living herds of starving things, and then to burst forth from the priory in that historic orgy of devastation which the peasants will never forget.

God, those carrion black pits of sawed, picked bones and opened skulls! Those nightmare chasms choked with the pithecanthropoid, Celtic, Roman, and English bones of countless unhallowed centuries! Some of them were full, and none can say how deep they had once been. Others were still bottomless to our searchlights, and peopled by unnamable fancies. What, I thought, of the hapless rats that stumbled into such traps amidst the blackness of their quests in this grisly Tartarus?

One time my foot slipped near a horribly yawning brink, and I had a moment of ecstatic fear. I must have been musing a long time, for I could not see any of the party but plump Capt. Norrys. Then there came a sound from that inky, boundless, farther distance that I thought I knew, and I saw my old black cat dart past me like a winged Egyptian god, straight into the illimitable gulf of the unknown.

But I was not far behind, for there was no doubt after another second. It was the eldritch scurrying of those fiend-born rats, always questing for new horrors, and determined to lead me on even unto those grinning caverns of earth's center where Nyar-lathotep, the mad faceless god, howls blindly in the darkness to the piping of two amorphous idiot flute-players.

My searchlight went out but still I ran. I heard voices, yowls, and echoes. But above all there gently rose that impious, insidious scurrying, gently rising like a stiff-bloated corpse gently rises above an oily river that flows under the endless onyx bridges to a black, putrid sea.

Something bumped into me—something soft and plump. It must have been the rats, the viscous, gelatinous, ravenous army that would feast on the dead and the living. Why shouldn't rats eat a de la Poer as a de la Poer eats forbidden things? The war ate my boy, damn them all, and the Yanks ate Carfax with flames and burnt Grandsire Delapore and the secret.

No, no, I tell you, I am not that demon swineherd in the grotto! It was not Edward Norrys' fat face on that flabby fungous thing! Who says I am a de la Poer? He lived, but my boy died! Shall a Norrys hold the land of a de la Poer? It's voodoo, I tell you...that spotted snake... Curse you, Thornton, I'll teach you to faint at what my family do! *'Sblood, thou stinkard, I'll learn ye how to gust...wolde ye swynke me thilke wys?...Magna Mater! Magna Mater!...Atys...Dia ad aghaidh's ad aodaun...agus bas dunarch ort! Dhonas 's dholas ort, agus leat-sa!...Ungl unl...rrlh...chchch...*

This is what they say I said when they found me in the blackness after three hours, found me crouching in the blackness over the plump, half-eaten body of Capt. Norrys, with my cat leaping and tearing at my throat.

Now they have blown up Exham Priory, taken my Nigel away from me, and shut me into this barred room at Hanwell with fearful whispers about my heredity and experience.

Thornton is in the next room, but they prevent me from talking to him. They are trying to suppress most of the facts concerning the priory, too.

When I speak of poor Norrys they accuse me of this hideous thing called murder, but they must know that I did not do it. They must know it was the rats, the slithering scurrying rats whose scampering will never let me sleep. The demon rats that race behind the padding in my room and beckon me down to greater horrors than I have ever known.

The rats they can never hear.

The rats in the walls.

HURRICANE LISA

R P STEEVES

The hunger nibbled at the inside of Anthony Rizzo's stomach, Riz to his friends—biting and clawing at his innards, burning away his intestines even as he tried to swallow, his spittle grinding at the raw redness of his throat.

Pumpkin pie, he thought. Sewer rat tastes like pumpkin pie.

No. Wait. That wasn't real. That was a joke, a line in a movie; a jheri-curled jester making light of diner food or something. He thought again, harder this time.

Forming a coherent thought was like pushing against thick velvet curtains in a stiff breeze. He kept getting turned around and trapped within the folds of half-formed memories.

Those fellas on that island. On that game show. They ate rats. Skewered 'em right up and gnawed on 'em like fried chicken from the Colonel.

Extra tasty crispy.

Riz stared at the rat in front of him, as he crouched low on the cold, concrete floor, but the creature seemed oblivious to his very presence.

This critter was nothing like the rat in that cartoon, the one that talked and cooked while riding inside that kid's hat. It didn't look plump or juicy, nor did it appear to be particularly intelligent, like those rats from that other cartoon movie, the one based on the kids' book or whatever. In fact, the scrawny sucker was just sitting there, nibbling on a piece of wire, oblivious to the world.

Much like Riz himself.

Like Riz, this particular rat was emaciated and dirty, all matted hair stretched over angular bones. But still it was the most delicious morsel Riz had seen in his entire sorry life.

The rodent in question had focused its attention on one of the damp, dirty corners of the dilapidated basement, zeroing in on an apparently fascinating pile of filth and rubble. Riz hadn't had much of a chance to investigate the room when he'd arrived in the grayest hours of the morning. He'd been far too busy fleeing the whipping wind and the ripping rain.

The door of the dilapidated cottage had been easy enough to break down and the floor, though filled with holes and sketchy in many places, had seemed more or less steady under his feet. Still, he'd headed to the basement almost immediately, figuring it to be the safest location in the abandoned home, and the best protection from the storm. He might have been a bit foggy in the head, but his survival instincts had kept him alive, in spite of what his lucid mind might fervently desire.

It had been far too dark in the basement for him to see any-thing clearly, but Riz had heard the scrabble of tiny feet and claws as he'd settled into one corner with his filthy blanket and his balled-up hoodie as a pillow. He'd had his usual dreams over-night: urgent plans and a sequence of numbers he couldn't quite manage to figure out in time; fevered presses of bodies, and women's faces with inscrutable expressions and falling—ever falling.

He'd awoken from his brief, fitful sleep famished and staring eye-to-beady-eye with the rodent.

Suddenly, without even realizing what he was doing, Riz sprung up, shooting across the room, crossing the space between man and rat with an alacrity that would have surprised him if he'd been cogent enough to comprehend his actions. As he leapt, the rat, sensing impending danger like some kind of rodent super-hero, valiantly attempted to flee, taking one small stride toward the foul-smelling sump in the far corner. But Riz was too fast for the creature.

He grabbed the rat in one swift motion, gripping it in one scabby, filthy hand, and in a savage surge of strength, snapped its pitiful neck. He raised the small carcass to his lips and tore his teeth into its flesh. As the blood ran free down his chin, he felt himself smiling with a bloated satisfaction he had never felt before.

Riz leaned against the rusted, long-dead water heater, sated for the first time in memory. As he rested, his senses took in more of his surroundings. The basement was lit by a faint, gray light streaming through the tiniest of windows set in the wall above his head. Through the cracked glass he could hear the wind tearing across the land; intermittently, slashes of sideways rain would slice through the holes in the glass.

The basement wasn't as bare as he'd thought upon first arriving. Most abandoned buildings he found in this decrepit region were in far worse shape. The entire area had once been a semi-popular vacation destination for wealthy weekenders from the Big City, a Paradise amusement park for small children and lovers of the beach.

But now it was just a wasteland, a post-apocalyptic bastion of refuse and ruined dreams. The carousel that had once brought pleasure to so many was a boarded-up, part-time crack den and the summer homes, like the one Riz was squatting in, were shambling shells of a happier time, now claimed by rot and rats, decay and desperation.

Like Riz himself.

The wind and rain had driven Riz to the small cottage, to feast on rats and search the basement for something, anything to dull the pain, even if only a little. The pain had been with him for so long. From the moment she'd left him, it had been a swift descent. First the drinking, mostly gin and sherry, but then whatever else he could scrounge up. Then came the shaking hands. Eventually, he couldn't hold a pen any longer, so his livelihood as a comic book inker had dried up faster than his ex-wife's sex drive.

Then he'd lost his health insurance, his mind, and finally, his home.

All he had now were the rats.

He could see them, skittering around at the edges of the basement, the corners of his vision filled with gray and brown rodents, his ears scraped raw with the sounds of their sharp claws rattling on the concrete.

He had to do something or he'd go mad. Well, madder.

Riz willed himself to rise, his body creaking and protesting. He would do what he did best now: scavenge.

On the other side of the rusted water heater was a shelving unit: gray, plastic and prefab. A mildewed cardboard box rested on the top shelf. With great effort, he dragged it down, accidentally smashing it onto his own head in the process.

He hardly felt a thing.

When he folded back the rotting flaps, he could scarcely believe his eyes. It was the jackpot he'd been waiting for since he had started this sorry journey months—had it only been months?—earlier.

It was a box full of booze. Sweet, numbing booze.

There were a few other things inside too. A wind-up radio, a moldy picture album, a few socks and oven mitts. But there were half a dozen bottles of alcohol, and it was the most beautiful sight he'd ever laid eyes upon.

He sat cross-legged on the floor and ritualistically unpacked the contents of the box.

A half-empty bottle of amaretto, two bottles of whiskey, a nearly drained fifth of scotch, and to his delight, both gin and vermouth.

He'd just have to imagine the olives.

He cradled one ice-blue bottle as if it was the baby he'd never been able to give his ex-wife.

Lisa. He forced himself to think her name, even if he couldn't speak it. *Lisa 'Marx,' now.*

Every time his mind returned to this darkened track, it started a spiral, an endless roller coaster loop-the-loop of repetitive thoughts. Bleak, soul-churning thoughts.

Luckily, there was one surefire way to cease those thoughts. Riz grabbed the radio and turned the crank furiously, channeling all the rage and bitter disappointment he could muster into powering the device. He fine-tuned the receiver to an oldies station, and to the minor chords of a song about broken hearts, he settled back onto his filthy blanket and slurped whiskey until the velvety folds of oblivion enveloped him.

The benefit of a booze-induced blackout was the banishment of the dreams. But as Riz roused from his slumber, his disorientation was evident. He must have been dreaming, of course, for the needle-sharp pains in his bare feet couldn't be real.

Had he even taken off his boots?

He supposed he must have, though he couldn't recall when. But that thought was banished from his mind as the shards of pain finally broke through the fog of alcohol and depression.

"Ow!" he screamed as he scuttled backward, smashing his head against the concrete wall, forcing his eyes open into the blinding pain that filled his vision. He shook off the stars and looked down at his bare feet, covered in a film of dirt, corns and scabs. They were being feasted upon by a half dozen desperate rats, tearing into Riz' flesh like pigs from a trough.

Riz screamed and flailed his legs, kicking his feet out in an attempt to shake off the vermin. They clung on tight with their sharp teeth, but Riz's desperation fueled his frantic strength, and he was able to cast them away, scattering the rats to the far corners of the basement. The rodents, their mouths stained with Riz's blood, scurried off toward the sump, disappearing down the hole before Riz could even release the breath he didn't know he was holding. He let it out in one, low whine, which had welled up from the depths of his inner darkness and shook his body as it passed through his lips. He looked down at the blood coursing from the wounds in his feet and shuddered at the violation.

The wounds were ragged smiles on his flesh; his fevered mind could almost feel the germs dancing along the edges, ready to dive into his being and surf through his veins. He grabbed the whiskey and splashed it onto his aching feet.

He screamed in agony as his flesh burned. But he had brought the suffering upon himself, and biting his lip, and drawing blood, he took a sharp breath through his nose. The pain was cleansing and he deserved it.

Slowly, he reached for his filthy hoodie, tearing strips from the ragged edges, then wrapped them around his tender feet. He settled down, his back against the cold concrete wall, and reached for the nearest bottle. He uncapped the scotch and took a swig, as the sound of the wind and rain echoed in his skull.

The radio had, apparently, run down. He picked it up and wound the crank, slower this time, as if the effort to do so was beyond his pitiful reserves. The only sustenance he could recall ingesting in the past week was the rat flesh he'd feasted on earlier. Then of course, the rats had feasted on him. It was, he thought bitterly, an apt depiction of the circle of life—or something.

As he finished cranking, the radio sprung to life, but rather than the dulcet tones of Motown, Riz heard instead, the monotone voice of a drone newscaster, dumping information on the captive listener.

"…tional Weather Service recommends that citizens take these evacuation orders seriously. Those living along the coastline, stretching from Paradise Beach to the tip of Native Cove, need to leave their homes immediately. In addition to the category four winds and the torrential rain, the rising tides threaten to flood the entire coastline. Reports state that this storm is shaping up to be the worst of the decade. Stay tuned to WLMC for updates on Hurricane Lisa."

With the utterance of that word, Riz hoisted the radio over his shoulder, ready to toss it across the room. He hoped it would shatter against the wall, symbolically destroying the name that had caused him such grief in the past year.

Lisa.

Of course the storm would share a name with his ex-wife. She had shown such a proclivity for destruction that he'd often considered her a force of nature.

The thoughts swept through him again, and he slumped down once more, the radio falling to the side and rolling toward the sump.

She had wrecked his life—his self-esteem, his career, and his heart. No, that wasn't entirely true. It had been his fault, and he'd come to realize this. He was the one who hadn't been good enough for her. Not charming or smart enough. Not a good enough listener. Not good enough in bed. He'd been moody and violent, self-destructive and suicidal. He'd begged her to stay, even threatened to kill himself if she left him. But she had done so nevertheless. Her new husband was, of course, better than Riz in every way. Bigger, stronger, better looking. He was a soldier and a war hero, with a house and a car and a high-paying job. Riz was nothing. Less than nothing. He was a vermin existing on the fringes of society, here in the basement with his brethren.

Those brethren were starting to make their presence known, too. Riz glanced over at the sump and saw a steady stream of water flowing from it. Along with the water came a pack of rats. A dozen or so, twice the number he'd seen to this point.

As the wind whipped outside and the sideways rain slashed through the broken window, Riz felt a chill ripple through his body. He had to get out of here. Hurricane Lisa was ravaging Paradise Beach, and the former amusement park wouldn't survive the floods and the wind. He knew this in his soul, and if the whole area wouldn't survive, neither could he. Even though he had lost everything when he'd lost her, he hadn't lost the will to survive, in spite of himself. He would continue to scavenge and scrounge, finding his home in the dirt on the bottom of the world.

He dodged past a pair of rats who were keen to feast on the wet cardboard box as he moved toward the stairs.

The rats on the floor numbered closer to two dozen now.

Riz put his bandaged foot on the bottom step. It was rough and cold. He willed himself to put his second foot on the next step. This was how he would make it up to the surface, with all his effort focused on one step at a time.

He'd reached the third step when it happened. The world shook and came tumbling down.

The fury of Hurricane Lisa reached a fever pitch at that moment. The winds rattled the cottage above him, and the small windows in the basement shattered, sending a spray of fine shards toward the floor now nearly covered with rats.

But more significantly, the cottage above crumbled and fell. The power of Lisa took it down—the once sturdy structure, a bright summer home that had housed families and children who had been excited about the carousel and a day at the beach. It toppled to the ground in one heaving, screaming instant. The crash was deafening and it knocked Riz down the two steps and onto the frigid, unyielding concrete floor.

The rotted and wooden stairs themselves succumbed seconds later, toppling down onto Riz in a shower of splinters and shards. For the second time in mere hours, stars danced in front of his eyes, as agony spidered through his brain. The wind was forced from his lungs, and he gasped for air, sharp jolts of pain spiking his chest as he did so.

After a few moments, he was able to force the shattered remains of the staircase off his body and he rose, shakily, to his feet. His body was now as broken, battered and bruised as his heart, but he wasn't dead.

At least, not yet.

But as Hurricane Lisa rained down her wrath on the world above, she also made her presence known in the darkened depths of the cottage.

Riz heard it first, the steady flow of water. Then he glanced at the sump and saw the geyser pouring forth from it. The rain and rising tides had affected the water table, raising it up; now it was flooding the basement.

In and of itself, that might not have been too bad. But unfortunately, it had other consequences. The rats that had been firmly ensconced in the bowels of the basement were now displaced, and they had fled to find succor. They were here in the basement.

And there were hundreds of them.

The first dozen had turned into two and then ten, then many more. They were everywhere. The floor, which had once been only dirty concrete, was now a living, writhing mass of fur, flesh and filth. The noise from the frightened rodents soon reached a crescendo, threatening to drown out the howl of Hurricane Lisa, and it was possible that the fury of the vermin might trump the power of Mother Nature herself.

Riz couldn't move. He was paralyzed with fear. The rats were panicking, wet and scared and angry. They ripped into each other, their hunger and fear driving them into a frenzy.

But they could sense something else. Perhaps it was the bloody rags on his feet. Perhaps it was the fear, desperation and loneliness in his soul. Perhaps they sensed a kindred spirit, one that was lost, afraid and unloved by the world at large. But undoubtedly, they sensed his vulnerability. They knew he was trapped, alone and defenseless, faced with their sheer number.

They turned as one, hundreds of tiny ears, beady eyes and sharp teeth rotating toward him. Their rage and hunger fell into synch, waves of desperation amplifying each other as their collective mob mentality told them to attack, to devour their prey, to fuel their survival as a species, to show the hurricane above that they, too, were a force of nature, one that couldn't be stopped, one that would take the heart of poor Anthony Rizzo and tear it to pieces.

He stood in silence, unmoving, as the tsunami of rats advanced on him, and as their needle-like teeth tore into his flesh even as the wind outside destroyed the once-proud Paradise Beach Amusement Park, he felt no pain.

While he was being consumed by the horde, digested into their collective being, all he could think about as he passed on from this world to the next was one single word:

Lisa.

LANDFILL BUFFET

A. P. FUCHS

The foul stench of rotting garbage made Nate Wendell throw up for the third time. He was on his back at the bottom of a garbage heap, and the most he could to do to let it all out was twist to his right and let it go. He was trapped under an enormous industrial refrigerator, pinning him from the hips down. The thing was one of those industrial fridges and weighed a ton. Despite sitting up and trying to move it off his legs, he couldn't make the thing budge. Its door faced the sky, the handle on the side furthest from him.

He'd been lying here for two days. He'd never been to the city dump before so could only assume he was in some forgotten corner away from the workers that he heard shouting every so often during daylight hours, always somewhere behind him and off to the right. No one answered his cries for help.

Now, it was night, the sky above overcast, a faint glow of gray light covering the garbage dump, making the piles of refuse appear like mountains of coal and volcanic ash. His legs had gone to sleep not long after he came to. If something was broken, he didn't feel it, but there'd been this insane, fiery pain rifling through his thighs and shins for a few hours there the other day. Then it faded and he was just numb, but not from the cold. The chill of the air was welcome, actually, the occasional rush of goose bumps across his skin a reminder he was still alive and his body still functioned despite the weight on his legs.

"You really got yourself into a big mess this time, didn't you?" he whispered to himself.

It wasn't supposed to be like this. He'd asked a small payday loan place on the corner for a tiny loan, some hundred and fifty dollars so he could buy a nice bike for his daughter. He borrowed the money, got the bike, and stashed it beneath a tarp in the garage. It was supposed to be revealed tomorrow, his daughter's birthday.

On payday a couple of days ago, he went to the loan place and promptly repaid the loan.

It was the shouting in the backroom that got his attention. The clerk at the front desk—a strawberry blonde with blue eyes—looked at him, clearly worried. When loud banging replaced the shouting, Nate went through the short gate on the other side of the clerk's counter and headed back there. He didn't know what he was thinking. Perhaps his instinct to help others and preserve the peace took over. That was why he had tried out being a cop several years back. He didn't make it through the testing and was devastated and ended up having to Joe job it at cardboard box manufacturing joint across town.

When he entered the back room, he was horrified to find some guy with his face planted against a desk, another guy standing behind him bending his arm behind his back, the other holding a gun.

What kind of place was this? He had thought these borrow-until-payday joints were safe. Who funded this joint? He didn't want to know.

The strength ran from his legs as the fight-or-flight instinct kicked in. The large man, the one with the gun, was on him before he could even take a breath to say something. A loud *thud* echoed inside his skull and somewhere beyond the darkness a gun went off.

He woke up at the dump.

That was two days ago.

Weak from no food or water, Nate tried once more to shove the fridge off himself. Nothing, no movement.

It was hopeless.

All he could do was wait out the night—*again*—and hope he could get someone's attention come morning.

With nothing to do, he crossed his arms over his chest, shivered, and closed his eyes. He was tired as it was. Sleep would pass the time nicely.

As he lay there, he let his mind wander to the morning. Someone would come. They'd get him out from under this fridge and, if his legs weren't damaged, he could make his way home, and see his daughter on her birthday.

See his wife, Dana.

Dana. She must be worried sick right now. She would've called the police after he didn't return home the other night, and if for some reason she didn't, she most certainly would've called them the next day when he didn't get home from work. Were the cops looking for him now? How long did it take? Aren't police supposed to be some kind of superheroes and when someone was in trouble come to their rescue? Were the guys who did this to him mob-related? Did they tip off the cops to ignore any reports of a missing forty-something?

It was impossible to know. Those guys had gotten the jump on him so quick.

Letting out a scream that did little but temporarily make him feel better, Nate tried to relax and let sleep take him. The foul smell of the rotten garbage threatened to make him throw up again, but without having put anything into his system for the past two days, he doubted he had anything left to yack out. And he hated the dry heaves so he hoped those wouldn't claim him either.

Loose garbage rustled to his right.

His eyes shot open and he looked in that direction. Nothing but a Coke can, a heap of black garbage bags, some loose papers, and slime.

He gazed back up at the sky, took a breath of the stinky night air, exhaled slowly and closed his eyes again.

More rustling, this time of thin plastic. He looked in the bags' direction again. Between the shadows filling every nook and cranny and the black garbage bags themselves, it was impossible to see much of anything.

He closed his eyes again for all of two seconds before a series of little squeaks immediately made them snap open. He *knew* that sound: mice. He'd had mice in his house before and heard them squeak and squeal whenever they got roiled up.

As long as they don't come over here then that's fine, he thought. Mice were relatively harmless. Leave them alone and they left you alone. Don't touch them; they were dirty and carried disease. Simple.

But it'd been *simple* that got him into this mess.

Knowing my luck, they'll start climbing all over me to check me out. Just don't breathe when they do. Lay still. Aw, shut up, man! You're freaking yourself out!

Nate waited for the squeaking and rustling to resume, but it never did. Finally calm enough to try and relax again, he closed his eyes and let himself doze off.

Shortly after, the squeaking returned, and it sounded like more than one mouse this time—and it sounded louder.

Nate froze. *Just. Lay. Still.* Mice weren't so bad, but the thought of them coming over to him and possibly crawling on him gave him the creeps. The garbage bags off to the side rustled again and despite the shadows he thought they moved slightly as well.

That's when he saw the shadow dart from out between two bags, come straight for him, leap over his chest and disappear into a heap of refuse on the other side.

"That was a *biiiiig* mouse," he whispered.

All was quiet again until a short time later and the bags started making noise, louder and more forced. It sounded like something was *in* the bag instead of merely scampering around outside it. Nate watched the bag and, sure enough, it began to pulse, something the size of a fist punching against it from within. For the briefest moment, he thought it was a body, some poor schlub who had gotten himself in deep just like he had and, like him, had been condemned to imprisonment at the city dump.

The garbage bag pulsed and shook.

Then went still.

From the other side, more movement and the crunching of torn paper. A shadow almost as long as Nate's forearm darted from around one pile of junk and in behind another before reappearing again and running at him. Like the one before, it leaped over his chest and disappeared between a mound of garbage bags.

"That was no mouse," Nate said. It was too big, at least a foot long. It was so hard to tell its exact size due to the limited lighting, but there was no way that was a run-of-the-mill mouse.

The rapid light taps of something hitting the filth on the ground on his left caught his attention, and when he turned his head he saw three large rats quickly bolting toward him. The three kept side-by-side, a parade of rodent pride. They slowed as they neared him, then stopped a mere six inches away.

"Go on, get out of here!" Nate screamed.

The rats' bodies twitched at the noise but they remained where they were.

"I said get out of here!"

For a moment he thought they would scamper off, but they didn't and instead came closer. One hopped onto his chest, which Nate quickly batted away. The little bugger nipped at his finger in the process and the sharp pinch of its teeth piercing his skin caused him to call out.

The second rat went straight for Nate's head, its tiny claws digging into his scalp. He swatted it away, cursing at it. The third was on his stomach, trying to dig through his shirt with its tiny claws.

Nate went to strike it, but one of the rats he'd batted away had run back and got on his hand, biting into his skin. Nate's eyes widened from the sudden sharp pain. He shook his hand to get the rat off, but the thing had wrapped its furry little body around his palm so tight he had to use his other hand to pry it off. He ripped the rat away, tearing skin from his hand in the process. Bleeding, he readied for another attack. Two of the rats ran around him, as if scouting a new route of assault. They disappeared behind the fridge on his legs and reappeared on the top of it a moment later. He didn't know where the third went.

The two rats jumped down and landed on him. He shot up, sitting upright, his hip bones pinned beneath the fridge lighting up with a jolt of pain from the movement. The rats rolled down his chest and into his lap. A sudden, aching shot of numbness rushed through his lower limbs. Did he somehow just jostle the fridge and his fast-asleep legs had reacted to it? He pounded against the fridge with his fists, trying to make it move. It rocked a little, but that was all.

The two rats nipped at his waist, biting through the band of his cotton pants. A sharp pinch sprouted up close to his gut and he saw the third rat digging into his shirt with its teeth. With a grunt, Nate wrapped his fingers around the rat, squeezed hard so it wouldn't escape his grip, and raised his hand high before bringing it down on the dirt beside him. The rat squealed on impact, its shrieks driving its comrades into a frenzy because they immediately went for the hand holding the rat.

Were rats smart enough to come to an ailing rodent's rescue? He didn't care and, ignoring the sharp pinches of rat teeth digging into his outer palm, he smashed the rodent against the dirt one more time for good measure. The creature didn't move when he let it go. He shook the other rat off his hand and readied himself to do the same to it and its friend when they got close enough.

The two rats eyed him and then leaped. One came straight for his face and latched on with its claws. He yanked it off, squeezing the thing so hard he felt its tiny ribs crack between his fingers. Like the other, he brought his hand high then took the rat to task against the dirt, ending it. The final rat bit and clawed at his midsection. Swiftly bringing his palms together in a harsh clap, he trapped the rat between his palms and crushed it. Bits of rodent guts and blood squirted out between his fingers.

Sitting there, catching his breath from the ordeal, sharp pricks of pain dotted his upper body where the little buggers had bit him; Nate yelled at the night sky.

"I can't believe this," he said. "Help!"

The garbage dump was quiet.

With a growl, he snapped out both palms and struck the fridge again, once more trying to move it. Like before, it rocked a little, but that was it.

That fresh and harsh tingling sensation powered through his legs and it felt like a full blown onslaught of pins and needles. Had he *actually* moved the fridge enough to allow blood flow into his legs, thus the sensation?

"Oh please, let it be so," he said.

He inhaled deeply then let out a loud exhale, coughing at the end of it. He listened intently for any more rats.

"Don't come near me! I'll kill you!"

Mouth dry, he twisted his lips and rolled his tongue around inside his mouth, trying to conjure up some moisture. After so long without water, all he got was a tiny drop of saliva. He wanted to spit it out and dispel the foul taste in his mouth, but decided to conserve it. Every drop counted right now.

The crunching of plastic made his ears perk up, same with the rustling of more garbage bags.

"Oh no, not again," he said.

The stench of rot made him wrinkle his nose and…what was that? A new smell? Something like a cross between a wet dog and rotten chicken.

Loud *thunks* brought his attention in front of him. Standing over him on top of the fridge was a large shadow. It looked like a cat.

"Oh good, you can chase the rats away," Nate said.

The cat looked at him. There was something strange about its eyes. They didn't reflect the light like a cat's normally did.

"Are you smart enough to go get help?" he asked. "No, you're a cat. You can't understand a word I'm saying, can you?" *Cats are useless.*

Beside the cat two more shadows emerged, both a little smaller. Kittens? Despite being pinned by a giant fridge and having nearly been gnawed to pieces by a few rats, Nate felt bad for the strays looking down on him. Poor thing had to take care of itself and its young in the dump.

"Sorry, don't got no food," he said. "Go on, look around here. I'm sure you'll find something. Probably sucks, whatever it is, but rotten fish is better than no fish, I suppose."

The three shadows remained facing him. One turned its head and the light of the moon glinted off its onyx eye. It face was far too long and narrow to be a cat's. Was that a pointy nose? It turned its head back and the moonlight caught it again. Its front teeth stuck out from beneath its top lip.

"That's no cat…" Nate said.

How a rat got so big, he had no idea and it didn't matter right now. As if the giant rodent knew he understood what it was, it leaped off the fridge and landed on his chest, knocking him flat on his back again. The thing weighed a solid fifteen pounds or more. Baring its teeth, the rat hissed and shoved its face into his, biting his lip. It caught on and pulled hard, tearing a chunk of it away. Blood gushed onto his chin.

"What the…"

The other two rats jumped off the fridge and landed on his stomach; both slowly walked up his body. He suddenly felt like the three small rats that had come before were just a warning of the nightmare he was now forced to endure.

The big rat dove in for another mouthful, this time punching its head through his clamped-shut mouth, and biting Nate's tongue.

Nate brought his fists in from the side and pounded on it. The thing pulled and pulled, tearing off a chunk of his tongue just as he knocked it off him. The other two ripped and clawed at his midsection, biting in and making quick work of tearing up his shirt. The warm trickles of blood leaked down either side of his body, their heat sending a quick wave of goose bumps through him before panic took over and heat encompassed his whole body.

"Help!" he shrieked, blood bubbling out of his mouth. What was left of his tongue felt like it was on fire.

His legs lit up with that same numb sensation as more and more rats piled onto the top of the fridge, their tiny bodyweights quickly adding up and putting more pressure on his legs.

Nate opened his mouth to cry out for help again, but the big rat quickly silenced him as it darted in and made for his tongue once more. It buried its head deep in his mouth, causing him to cough and gag on its furry skull. The taste of it brought the little that was left in his stomach all the way to the top floor, filling up the back of his throat as he lay there, arms flailing, one rat biting and chomping at his tongue, two others eating away at his gut.

The horde of rodents on top of the fridge dove off, cascading over the side of the fridge like a black, oily waterfall. They covered his body, their weight enough to cause him to panic even more, his arms now useless at his sides.

Squeezing his eyes shut, letting loose a muffled scream against the rat in his mouth, his lungs pounding for air, Nate tried to sit up, but couldn't muster the strength to do it.

Sharp pains shot through his flesh with each bite the rats took. His heart ran at a hundred miles a minute, drumming so hard it filled his ears.

Warm blood coated his limbs, ran down his sides, oozed out of his mouth and he knew he was moments away from passing out.

The tiny shrieks and squeaks of the rats reached a cacophony of squealy sound.

From behind, a dog barked, hoarse and loud. The rats squealed and their weight began to dissipate off him. The one in his mouth was yanked out and when Nate opened his eyes, he saw through blurry vision a big brown and black German shepherd making quick work of the enormous rat between its powerful jaws.

Heavy footfalls rose up behind him, boots crunching on dirt. They stopped. "Hey, fella, you all right?"

Nate's eyes were so filled with tears and blood he could hardly see the older gentlemen in the baseball cap looming over him. Nate tried to speak but only blood gurgled out between his lips. His lungs ached for air and the most he could manage were small sips through his nostrils.

"What happened here?" the old man said slowly.

The dog growled.

The old man must have noticed the fridge and shone his flashlight at it. "You mean you're trapped under there?"

Nate could barely nod his head.

The old man went over to the fridge. "Do you want I should push it?"

He wanted to tell the old man he'd tried. He tried for two days and couldn't get the thing to move.

Where was this old man over the past forty-eight hours? Was he midnight security and had missed Nate somehow? Did the chorus of wild squeaks tip him off that something was going down in a forgotten corner of the garbage dump?

The old man pushed against the fridge, rocking it. Nate didn't think it was a good idea. If his legs were broken beneath, moving the fridge would only make things worse. Then again, he had tried moving it himself. Besides, he could barely feel anything except the occasional rush of pain.

The old man rounded to the far side of the fridge and opened its door. All Nate could make out from the other side was, "Oh son…oh no…there's this hole here and…"

Rats poured out of the fridge, climbing out over the sides, landing on the ground to the left and right.

Through hazy vision, Nate watched as the swarm drew closer and closer to him.

The big dog growled and barked at the rats. The rodents didn't back down. The old man came round about the fridge, stomping on the ground, squishing some of them under heel and bouncing around like a man riding a bull.

Plastic garbage bags rustled. More shadows crept in from the sides. Others scampered down the mounds of garbage like the cavalry coming down to do battle in the valley.

The dog swiped and pawed at the rats. They climbed up the canine's body and mounted its back. Others climbed up the old man's legs. He ran over to Nate, shoved the flashlight into his mouth, and squatted down behind him.

"We got to get out of here, son." He scooped his arms under Nate's shoulders and started to pull, apparently ignoring the rats climbing and coiling up his legs.

Nate wanted to call out, tell him to stop, that he was crazy to try and just simply pull him out from under the fridge.

The words never came. His mouth was too swollen and too full of blood to even talk. More and more rats poured out from between the mounds of garbage, covering Nate and the old man like bees over a honeycomb.

The old man pulled and Nate heard a wet rip come from somewhere down by his legs. He didn't have to see to know what happened. The fridge. The rats. The hole the old man said was in the fridge. The rats had somehow gotten inside and ate straight through his legs. The weight of the fridge had cut off his circulation, maybe even acted like some kind of weird tourniquet, numbing the whole thing except for the occasional nerve flare up. Now, with his body torn almost in two, it would just be moments until...

The old man had stopped pulling and Nate heard a thud behind him.

"Ar...y..." He wanted to ask, "Are you okay?" but knew he wouldn't get a reply. The rats had gotten to the old man. The dog—Nate couldn't see the dog anymore. He couldn't see much of anything anymore. Just shadows. Just oily, furry, squeaking shadows. All over his body.

Dizziness crept in and he couldn't see anything.

He'd be dead soon.

The blood loss would force him to pass out any moment. In the meantime, all he could do was feel the rats biting into him, eating him, turning him into some kind of landfill buffet.

ABOUT THE WRITERS

Mariah Deitrick is a wife, mother of four, and a writer. She's a graduate from the Institute of Children's Literature, and is the author of the adult novel, "Deadly Hunt," and the Young adult novel, "The Forgotten." Her work has appeared in a variety of markets including, Spaceports, Undead Press, and Spidersilk, Knowownder!, Super Teacher Worksheets, Stories That Lift, StoryTeller Tymes, and Living Dead Press.

A complete list of her work can be found at her website www.mariahdeitrick.weebly.com

Robert DuBuque lives in Massachusetts with his wife and daughter. He enjoys reading, writing, and mentally preparing for the apocalypse. When he's not writing he works as a mechanic and hangs out with his little girl.

A.P. Fuchs is the author of many novels and short stories, most of which have been published. His most recent books are "Redemption of the Dead," the third book in his zombie trilogy, "Undead World; Axiom-man: City of Ruin"; the paranormal romance series "Blood of my World" and "Zombie Fight Night: Battles of the Dead," in which zombies fight such classic monsters as werewolves, vampires, Bigfoot, and even go up against awesome foes like pirates, ninjas, and Bruce Lee.

Also a cartoonist, he's known for his superhero series, "The Axiom-man Saga," both in novel and comic book format.

Please see www.axiom-man.com for more on this series.

He lives and writes in Winnipeg, Manitoba, and barely ever leaves the house. Visit him on the Web at www.canisterx.com and follow him on Twitter at www.twitter.com/ap_fuchs

Anthony Giangregorio is the author of 48 novels and children's books, almost all of them about zombies, and has edited over 40 anthologies and books.

His work has appeared in Dead Science & Metahumans vs. the Undead by Coscomentertainment, Dead Worlds: Undead Stories Volumes 1-7, and Wolves of War by Library of the Living Dead Press. He also has stories in End of Days: An Apocalyptic Anthology Vol. 1-5, the Book of the Dead series Vol. 1-6 by LDP, Zombie Zoology by Severed Press, and two anthologies with Pill Hill Press. He's also the creator of the 10 book action/zombie series titled "Deadwater" and the apocalyptic series "Warriors of the Apocalypse." His action/horror novel "Dead Rage" is being optioned for a movie at this time.

Robert Ervin Howard (1906-1936) was an American author who wrote pulp fiction in a diverse range of genres. He's well known for his character Conan the Barbarian and is regarded as the father of the sword and sorcery subgenre. He was born and raised in the state of Texas.

Meagan Jeffrey is a mother of four beautiful children, who reside in Cambridge, Ontario Canada. She started writing in grade 2, when she wrote her first short story that won an Alberta wide short story competition for school-aged children. From there, she wrote poetry and won many contests, moved to writing short stories for magazines, short zombie stories that have been published with Living Dead Press, and most recently a novel about Marilyn Monroe.

H.P. Lovecraft was born on August 20, 1890, in Providence, Rhode Island. The horror magazine "Weird Tales" bought some of his stories in 1923. His story "The Call of Cthulhu" came out in 1928 in "Weird Tales." In his final years, he took editing and ghostwriting work to try to make ends meet. He died on March 15, 1937, in Providence, Rhode Island.

R P Steeves is a former teacher and a writer who specializes in the fantastic. His most recent novel, an urban fantasy tale of paranormal detection, "The National Maul" is now available in print and ebook formats, and is the second book in the Misty Johnson series.

Follow his blog and learn of his upcoming horror, fantasy, sci-fi and pulp adventure titles at http://www.rpsteeves.com

Abraham Stoker (1847-1912) was born in Dublin and is best remembered for his 1897 novel "Dracula."

Scott Wieczorek is a professional archaeologist who has authored numerous archaeological / historical studies. He's a newcomer to the world of published fiction despite his life-long interest in writing horror. He's recently finished his first novel, "Byron: A Zombie Tale" which was released in January 2013 and will be releasing his second novel, "Witness Through Time," in June 2013. He also operates a fiction blog featuring several ongoing tales and book reviews at wieczorekfictblog.blogspot.com.

Anthony Alexander Valade is an independent horror writer working out of Winnipeg, Manitoba Canada. He's had several poetic works published in a Zombie Anthology titled "Undead Tales 2." Check out his rich and psychedelic "Zombie Poetry" and short stories on Facebook at: ADiethylamide.

MORE HORROR FICTION BY STFU PUBLISHING!
THE CONSERVATORY
by Michele Roger

After lying dormant for years, the Hillford Conservatory curse has ris
from its blood-soaked foundations. A student's corpse is found in the river w
its arms cut off. A nurse at the local hospital is found dismembered while t
walls of the hospital bleed. Students at the Conservatory have night terrors
being attacked by tiny blue creatures with scalpels and drills.

Some students say they see and hear the voice of a recently deceased stude
as the ghost haunts the school. While the administration tries to save t
reputation of the elite music conservatory, the gruesome secrets of Hillfo
begin creeping out. But when a second student goes missing, it's up to L
Martin Lewis and music teacher Melody Steinwick to piece together the past
order to unravel the secrets of the present.

With death roaming the halls of Hillford, no one is safe.

DROPPING FEAR
by Mike Catalano

On a dark night 25 years ago, masked maniac Derek Haddonfear went o
a bloody rampage... Today, Derek's son, Will, is happily married, but still
struggles to distance himself from the harsh memory of his father. He and
his wife, Kerri, have been trying to get pregnant for years with zero success.
Infertility begins to take its toll on their marriage.

Kerri can't live without becoming a mother and Will can't live seeing his
wife so distraught. Upon coming into contact with a doctor working on an
experimental fertility drug, a desperate Will and Kerri decide to give him a
shot. What results from the procedure sends Kerri on an uncontrollably
violent path that is all too familiar to Will. Is it her hormones? Is it the drug
Or is Will's chilling past coming back to haunt him in the most bizarre of
fashions? Regardless, no one will be prepared for the birth of the newest an
most unexpected psychotic slasher in the history of horror.

DREAM WEAVERS: STORIES TO SCARE YOU
by Grady, Kate Yandell and Hope Yandell

Dream Weavers is a collection of stories that revolve around a commo
theme... dreams and nightmares. Within this book are tales to make you laug
cry and be chilled to the bone. Written by a family of scribes, these tales
skinwalkers, aliens and zombies, are sure to leave you wanting more. So tu
down the lights and get comfortable, but not too comfy, for what might
hidden in the shadows may be all too real.

THE CURSE OF THE BEETLE
by Anthony Giangregorio and Richard Marsh

Something evil stalks British politician Paul Lessingham through nineteenth century London. Neither a man nor a woman, the fiend hunts from the shadows, seeking vengeance for past deeds by mesmerizing others to do its bidding.

Lessingham is a haunted man, and though in fear for his life, it's possible the past is far more dangerous than the present. With the help of Sydney Atherton and Marjorie Lindon, he will attempt to escape the clutches of revenge. But can any man escape *The Curse of the Beetle?*

RANDY AND WALTER: KILLERS
by Tristan Slaughter

Randy Barcer lived his life the way he wanted to, joyfully slaughtering innocent women and children. But sometimes he did much worse to them and those that died would be considered the lucky ones. That is until he met Walter Brenemen, and he soon found out that this man who claimed to be his brother, was far more dangerous than Randy could ever hope to be. "I'll give you a name of a woman and tell you where to find her. Then we'll see which one of us can get to her first. If you win, I'll leave you alone. But if I win...well, I guess we'll just have to wait and see." With those words, Walter changed Randy's life forever. It was a simple game. Whoever kills the most, wins...with a small town caught in the middle. Welcome to a world of despair and suffering, torture and blood, but most of all...Death

MEN OF PERDITION
by Kelly M Hudson

They are five evil entities, born from the bowels of World War II and dark legends of the past. The Weeping Lady, The Mad Gasser, Spring-Heeled Jack, The Bone Sniffer, and their servants, the Black-Eyed Children. They descend upon the small town of Constance, Kentucky, to enact a ritual of horror and slaughter meant to drive mankind to its knees. Only a small group of humans, survivors of the night of terror, can stand between our world and the advent of theirs. Can this band of survivors stop the Men of Perdition, or will these foul creatures unleash a demonic evil of torture, torment, and terror upon the Earth? The battleground has been chosen and the players are few. Who can stop *The Men of Perdition?*

VICTORY OF THE DEAD
ANTHONY GIANGREGORIO

ETERNAL AFTERMATH

A ZOMBIE NOVEL

MICHAEL D. GRIFFITHS

www.ingramcontent.com/pod-product-compliance
Lightning Source LLC
Chambersburg PA
CBHW070502120726
47910CB00003B/1096